DWELLERS

DWELLERS

a novel

Eliza Victoria

TUTTLE Publishing

Tokyo | Rutland, Vermont | Singapore

Rule No. 1:

You don't kill the body you inhabit.

What.

PART ONE

A Strange House
in a Strange City

1

The Holmes and Rahe stress scale lists 43 stressful life events that may lead to illness. I read this in a book—being wheelchair-bound and injured I can do mostly nothing but read. Every life event has corresponding Life Change Units. This is my list—

Death of a close family member – 63
Personal injury or illness – 53
Change in living conditions – 25
Revision of personal habits – 24
Change in residence – 20
Change in sleeping habits – 16
Change in eating habits – 15

—for a whopping total of 216 Life Change Units. I don't know if I should add "Gaining a New Family Member" (39 points); I've known Louis (I should get used to calling him this name—*Louis*) all my life, but I've never shared a house with him. Does that count?

He stresses me out because he *looks* stressed out with all the cuts on his face and arms. His constant attention is breaking my heart. Maybe he could add the 39 points to his own list.

If I add that, I get 255 points, still 45 points short of the requisite 300, which means "at risk of illness". At this point, I'm still not at risk? "Risk of illness is moderate".

This is bullshit.

How many Life Change Units apply to a "Change in Body"? "Change in Residence" is a mere 20 points. A change in body is a thousand-fold more disorienting.

I don't know why I'm even bothering with this stress scale. It doesn't apply to Louis and me. Our collective stress is on a whole other planet.

I should be doing something more productive.

I wish I could walk.

I wish I could just kill this body and inhabit another.

2

I take stock of what I have, once again: male, medium build, early 20s, close to my real age. Dark hair. Dark eyes. My insides feel tender. Black wheelchair. My right leg stretched out in front of me, bound in a black knee immobilizer. The immobilizer looks expensive; it has a dial on the joint that you can adjust to control range of movement. Not that I have any range.

Dashboard knee. Nerve damage. Knee dislocation. *Posterior cruciate ligament injury.* The words make my head throb.

My other leg is covered in fading bruises, like swatches of paint. Mauve. Chartreuse. The sickly yellow of sulfur.

Louis said I was in a coma for two days. He himself woke up in the car wreck, ambulance sirens blaring in his ears. He was disoriented by the sudden change in position. From the SUV, he woke up in the driver's seat of a sedan, a car pinned between the SUV and a tree trunk. He looked through the car's accordioned backseat and saw our discarded bodies in the other vehicle. Then he saw this unconscious body on the passenger seat, saw the strange way the right leg was twisted, and thought I was dead.

"I thought it didn't work," he said, when I woke up on the hospital bed. He was holding my hand. He might have been crying. He let go of my fingers, patted my arm. "Rule No. 1," he said. "You don't kill the body you inhabit."

What.

"We can't do this again, Jonah."

But my legs are ruined, I wanted to say. *And who is Jonah?*

Rule No. 2:

You should never again mention your previous name.

Louis said that, for a few days after I woke up, I kept insisting that I got my knee injury from a bad fall. I climbed a tree, hung onto a branch for a few seconds and, inexplicably, let go.

Louis said I was so steadfast in this story, so unwavering, that when he began showing me the newspaper articles and photos of the car crash, I got angry.

I have no memory of this.

However, the story of my fall did happen. When I was younger, eight or nine, it was the mango tree my grandfather—

Rule No. 3:

You don't ever talk about your previous life.
Ever.

I should write down these rules in a proper fucking list and staple it to my damn forehead.

It is March, and I am in a city I don't recognize. My room is clean and bare, just filled with the essentials: a bed, a cabinet, a study table with a lamp, and a low bookshelf filled with books. A pair of aluminum crutches I still can't use leaning against a wall. The house is on an affluent street. Gated, with a driveway. The other houses stand practically side-by-side, but this house sits on a big lot, so the nearest house on either side is more than a hundred meters away. Craftsman-style bungalow. Attached garage. Gray-green brick walls. So muted it could very well blend into the trees. Wood and marble interior. There is even an attic and a basement. Or so Louis said. We've never lived in a house with an attic and a basement.

Obviously, I've never been on any other floor but this one. I'm not missing much, according to him. The attic is filled with boxes, and an old dresser cabinet has fallen over and blocked the basement stairs, so he can't explore much.

We don't have visitors or nosy neighbors, which is good. The other houses are quiet. Once or twice, I've seen a little girl looking at our house from the other side of the street. She seems to like playing dress-up. The first time I saw her she was wearing pink fairy wings. I thought I was hallucinating.

Bills come to the house in envelopes but Louis says all of the bills can be paid online. There is a desktop and a laptop in his room, the contents of which he has studied for days.

"What is your job?" I ask.

"IT professional," he says. "Independent consultants. We're partners, apparently."

"I don't know what that is." Meaning, I don't know how to pretend to be *that*.

He says it doesn't matter. "Based on the emails, the clients know we've been in a car accident. I don't think they'll bother us for a while."

Louis says I own two phones and a laptop, but they have been ruined in the crash.

A cleaning lady dropped by five days after I was released from the hospital. She seemed to know us quite well, based on the way she spoke to us, so Louis and I pretended that we knew her. She talked to us as if we were her children, as she wiped the windows and cleaned the refrigerator. Before she left in the afternoon, she took Louis's hands in hers and told him how kind he was to take care of his injured brother. Louis merely smiled because he didn't know her name. He said that we were letting her go. *The hospital bills,* Louis told her. *We need to save as much money as we can.* She was surprised, but said she understood.

The truth was we just didn't want to let anyone else into this house.

Every Monday an old man drops by with a week's worth of groceries. When Louis tried to pay him the first week we were in the house, the man laughed and said we were already paid for two months. The grocery comes in large blue plastic bags. Sometimes a teenager helps the old man. Maybe his son. There is always meat and vegetables, milk and fruits. They recycle. Cooking oil comes in plastic Coke bottles, vinegar in ketchup containers. The correct ingredients in incorrect vessels. Like Louis and me.

I wonder if the old man's been fired yet. Probably not. It's a great help, to have groceries delivered to your doorstep.

How far away are we, I have asked Louis once, and he said, nearly 300 miles.

Not far enough, I think.

I know Louis has put a protective spell around the house but he won't admit to it. I know because I saw it. My bedroom faces the street so I have a view of the gate from my window. One morning, while Louis was watering the bougainvillea bushes in the garden, I saw a girl—college student, maybe eighteen—walk up to the gate and ask, "Is Meryl here?"

She was wearing a pair of glasses with big black frames. Her hair was dyed a deep, dark magenta, but even the pop of color couldn't hide her weariness. Louis stopped watering the flowers.

"Who?"

"Meryl," she said.

"I'm sorry, I don't know who that is."

She raised her hand toward the gate, and I saw it then—a flicker of fear in her eyes. She lowered her hand. She looked confused. She stared at Louis as though begging him to explain what just happened.

13

"Yes?" Louis said. Taunting her. He couldn't help it. She stepped back and walked away.

"You shouldn't have done that," I said when Louis got back inside.

"What?" Louis said.

"The perimeter spell. You should conserve your energy."

"I wonder who Meryl is," was all Louis said.

It is a strange thing, to inhabit another body. I mourn the loss of my childhood scars and despise the wounds that have replaced them. The fall from the mango tree produced a hook-like scar on my elbow, a brown itch-less welt that I touch before I go to sleep. That hook is no longer there. Sometimes I still get surprised. In the dark, I do not recognize myself.

Jonah has scars of his own, but I don't know the stories behind them. I wonder if he was a good person.

Rule No. 4:

You shouldn't feel sorry for the life you've displaced.

3

ouis says he found three dead birds in the backyard. He picked up all three with a shovel and buried them in the garden.

"Remember when Grandfather got sick?" I tell him. "Three of his favorite dogs died, and then he got better. Like the dogs suffered his illness for him."

Rule No. 3. "Jonah," Louis says.

"Maybe I'll get better."

"You *will* get better."

"But those birds aren't mine. And Grandfather ended up dying anyway."

"What's wrong?"

I am in pain. I have just taken my medication but it has yet to take effect. I understand the importance of pain. It is the body's defense mechanism. Get burned and you learn to stay away from fire. But prolonged pain? What's the point?

I am injured—*I get it.* Why continue to make my body suffer?

Pain is bad for the heart, my mother used to say.

Louis offers his hand and I squeeze it, hard. I didn't know it was possible to suffer pain such as this.

"Maybe we are not who we think we are," I say, feeling delirious. "Maybe this is really my body."

"Stop it, Jonah."

But it hurts so much, I want to say, but there are things you don't say out loud to preserve your dignity.

Louis places an ice pack on my knee and sits with me until the wave of pain passes.

"What are we doing, Louis?" I say.

"Biding our time. Resting."

"We've stayed in one place for too long. We're sitting ducks."

"When you get better we'll move again." He takes a deep breath. "We haven't seen her. Maybe she doesn't know where we are."

"But what if I don't get better?"

"Stop thinking like that."

We fall silent. I see an image of a young girl sitting in a yellow kitchen, her back to me. Chair of blonde wood. Black dress, black hair, hands on her knees. I experience it like a flash, a burn. *Pain is bad for the heart.* I think of her name but don't say it out loud. A sacred word. *Celeste.*

"I'm sorry, Louis," I say.

"You didn't force me to help you," he says.

I think Louis thinks we are secluded and safe, as though he has already forgotten what real seclusion means and what my former life is like. (Look at me, breaking Rule No. 3 again.) The hush of a huge century-old ancestral house, surrounded by nothing but trees and fields, that's what seclusion is. At night, I still dream of gleaming wooden floors and capiz shells. The narrow passageways surround the living room and lead to the kitchen. I follow these passageways but cannot find their end.

4

There are two girls on a bed. One wears a white shirt—a man's shirt—and the other is naked, save for a pair of pink panties. They face a barred window. They are both kneeling on the bed. I am sitting in one corner of the room. I should be able to see their faces in profile but I can't. It is as though I am looking through a camera eye with the frame cut off. I can see them clearly from the chin down. The girl in the shirt touches the naked girl's breast, slides her palm down her bare stomach, and slides her fingers under the garter of her pink panties. Her free arm is around the naked girl's neck. The naked girl is trying to pull the other girl's arm down. The naked girl is crying.

I wake up and all of the lights are off. The clock reads 2 AM.

A dream. It is just a dream. I sit up. Normally I dream of the big house and Celeste. The twins. But this dream is different. It doesn't feel connected to me.

Louis steps into the room with a flashlight. "Blackout," he says, rubbing his eyes. He yawns. "The entire street is dark." He places the flashlight on the study table.

"I had a dream," I say.

Louis doesn't say anything except, "Hm," probably thinking he already knows what the dream is about.

"It's not about Celeste," I say.

"You shouldn't say her name," Louis says. He pulls out the chair from the study table and sits on it.

"There were two girls. I think one of them is sexually abusing the other."

"Jesus, Jonah."

Louis and I have talked about this exhaustively. We are what we remember. Or what we choose to remember. If we lose our memories, we lose ourselves. But where do memories reside? Are they tangible objects you find in the organic brain? Do you take them with you when you leave your body, or are they left with the corpus? Do they simply disappear, like steam? Or are they more like the boxes in the attic or the ruined dresser cabinet in the basement? Things that can be abandoned and later inherited.

"Do you think it's Jonah's memory?" I ask.

He yawned again. "Maybe."

"I hope Jonah is not a monster."

Louis laughs, to my surprise. "Maybe he just saw it in a movie. Online. Someplace. You find the most depraved things online."

That is possible. "I hope so," I say. "You're tired, Louis. Go back to sleep. Thanks for the flashlight."

"I hope the blackout ends soon," Louis says before he closes the door. "We have meat that might go bad."

There is still no electricity the next morning. I have cold coffee and bread and NSAIDs for breakfast. I wheel myself to the window to catch a breeze. No such luck. The humidity is unforgiving. I watch Louis stand near the bars of the gate and listen to a couple of women fanning themselves, neighbors commiserating, speculating on the cause of the power outage.

"Transformer blast," Louis reports back to me. It's too hot to do anything. Louis sits, languorous, on a chair in my room and stares at the ceiling. I hunch over a book. The skin covered by my knee immobilizer starts to sweat and itch. We don't talk. What is there to talk about when you can't talk about your past? *Remember that time when we had a power outage for two days, and we had dinner in the garden with all the grown-ups? We wore our best suits and felt like grown-ups ourselves.*

We can't talk about that.

We notice the smell around lunchtime. Louis has wheeled me out of the room into the dining area despite my protestations. Beef stew.

"I'm not hungry," I say.

"You need to eat something."

I haven't eaten much of anything ever since the hospital. Louis gives me a look. I sigh, pick up a spoonful of beef, eat it, and chew. It should be enough to placate him. He frowns. I try to eat more but cannot find pleasure in it. I have no appetite. My hands hang limp at the end of the wheelchair armrests. I watch Louis finish his meal.

That's when I notice it. A faint stench in the air, like rotten meat.

"Do you smell that?" I say.

Louis looks up. "I've used up all of our meat in the stew," Louis says, but enters the kitchen anyway to check.

"Well, it's not coming from the refrigerator," he says.

"But you do smell that, right?"

"Yes." He sits at the table again but stands up after a moment, agitated. "Shit. Where is that coming from?"

Louis places the dishes in the sink and leaves the dining room. I wait, listening to him walking around the house. He stops walking after a few minutes, but doesn't return to the room. I wheel myself out.

I find him in the laundry room, where the stench is stronger. It smells like leftover rice left out in the sun. The door leading to the basement is straight ahead. The plain white door has, in addition to the doorknob, a slide bolt latch that looks newer than the rest of the house. Louis unlatches the door and the smell hits us like a wave.

"Damn," I say, covering my nose with the collar of my shirt.

"What *is* that?" Louis says. "Did something die down there?"

I can see the dresser cabinet seven steps down, right at that point before the winding staircase turns.

"You can't go in there," I say. "You might get hurt."

Louis goes down the seven steps with a flashlight. "I still can't see anything," he says. He goes back up, sees me there and gives me a look as though seeing me for the first time. "Do you want to go back to your room?"

"I can wheel myself back you know," I say, slightly miffed. "And you're not going down there."

"I'll be careful," he says. He goes out, and disappears for a long time, and comes back with a hammer, safety goggles, and a pair of rubber boots.

"You have got to be kidding me," I say.

"I wish I had an ax," Louis says, putting on the goggles and the boots. He goes down the basement stairs.

"Why do you need to go investigate?"

"If there's a dead animal down there it's going to stink up the street."

I hear splintering wood, a boot crushing through a board. Louis curses. "You might cut yourself," I shout through the doorway. The hammer goes down. The glow of the flashlight disappears further down the staircase.

"Well?" I say. I hear squeaks against a cement floor.

"Old furniture," Louis says. He grunts. "It smells really bad down here."

"Dead cat?" I say.

"It smells like shit and bleach."

"Did you say 'bleach'?" I say, but Louis doesn't reply.

For a minute I couldn't hear anything. Then heavy footsteps, boots crashing through wood. Louis emerges from the dark basement, ashen-faced.

"What?" I ask, wheeling myself back. He puts down the flashlight and the hammer on the floor and slams the basement door shut. He pulls off the goggles and sits on the floor with his back to the door. He covers his face with both of his hands and tries to breathe.

I'm frightened. This is no dead cat.

"Louis?" I say, softly.

"Oh my God," Louis says, dropping his hands from his face. He looks at me. "There's a chest freezer down there."

My heart stops.

"There's a dead girl in it," Louis says.

5

Who are these people, really? Louis and Jonah—who are they? For the first time since we arrived in this house, I am disturbed by the lack of photos on the walls, the lack of framed certificates, words to live by, the lack of life.

The girl in the chest freezer is naked and emaciated, Louis tells me. Sunken cheeks, ribs poking through. Fingers like claws. She looks both old and young, at once a child and a grandmother. Louis finds it impossible to guess her age, though he immediately thinks of the words *anorexic* and *teenager*. She is concealed beneath melting blocks of ice.

Today marks the third week since I left the hospital. How long has she been in that freezer?

Who hid her there?

We puzzle over the detail of the fallen dresser cabinet. Someone went to the basement, toppled the cabinet over, and left how?

Louis says there is a large window over the freezer, large enough for an adult to crawl through. The glass panes have been painted over with brown paint. It's locked from the outside and leads into the backyard. All right: so, someone came from outside, toppled the cabinet over, and went back out the window? Clearly the cabinet was pushed to discourage people inside the house from exploring the basement.

"Is that why they were driving so fast?" I say. I remember us in the SUV. I remember the sedan with Louis and Jonah (though we didn't know their names then) zooming out of a street and appearing in front of us, suddenly in the way, suddenly giving us a way out of our old life.

They were driving fast because they were escaping the scene of a crime, a scene we have now inherited.

"We need to get out of here," I say.

We have moved back to the dining area. Louis is massaging his forehead. It is starting to get dark.

"We don't have a car," he says. "You are injured."

"But we can't stay here." It is starting to get dark and I am terrified.

"We wouldn't have known about the chest freezer if the electricity didn't go out."

"What are you saying?"

"If the power comes back, we'll be okay."

"And if it doesn't?"

"Then we'll go," Louis says. "But we are doomed if that's the case. A neighbor will call the police and report the smell. They will discover the body in the basement, and the man who delivers our groceries will be questioned and he'll tell the police who we are."

This damn body. This damn face.

Louis says, "We'll be on the run."

Again, I say in my head.

"And we can't really run that far."

"I can't believe this is happening," I say.

"I know."

"Isn't it ironic that I try to escape and I end up anyway in the body of a—"

"Don't," Louis says. "Just don't."

There comes a time when you just need to let the tears fall. To Louis's credit, he keeps his gaze averted, giving me some privacy. (Irrelevant, really, in my case, when I can't even give myself a bath or even hobble to the urinal by myself.)

"Maybe they didn't do it," he says. "Maybe Louis and Jonah are innocent."

The electricity comes back in the early evening, and I do not know whether to be relieved or alarmed.

We can't sleep. Though I have not seen the dead girl myself, Louis has described her to me, and this may be worse than actually seeing her in person. She looms large in my mind. I imagine her putrefaction, her skin sliding off her flesh and breaking open, putrid and green, and her eyes bulging as her body bloats with gases.

Louis goes up to the attic with a flashlight. I sit away from the opening, thinking he might start throwing boxes down the pull-down staircase.

"What exactly are you looking for?" I ask.

"I don't know," Louis says. "Clues."

He rattles around up there like the largest rat alive. Twenty minutes later, Louis comes back down, covered in sweat, cobwebs, and dust. He sees me and shakes his head. Nothing.

"Mostly old books and papers," he says. "But I haven't looked properly. It's too hot."

I wheel out to the living room and wait for Louis to finish washing his face and arms.

"What are you expecting to find?" I ask as he sinks into the sofa.

"Do you think she was killed here?" Louis asks.

"What?"

"If she was killed here," he says, "she might have left something. A bag. Shoes."

"She was naked, you said."

"Yes."

"Someone's already burned her clothes," I say. "Buried them. There are no more clues."

But we keep on searching, even as we go through the rest of our day. Louis is in the kitchen cooking but I can hear him opening all of the cupboards, I can hear him walking around the house as something simmers on the stove. I am in my room, ostensibly reading a new book, but I open the cabinet, pull open the shelves, and look through the detritus. We can't let it go. It's like an echo that keeps nagging at us.

There is a gap between the wall with the window and the back of the low bookshelf in my room.

To look behind the shelf, I have to crouch on the floor, sit up, and peek, or pull the shelf away from the wall. I can do none of these things.

I wheel myself to the door. "Louis!"

"What?" He sounds like he's in the laundry room again.

"Come over here for a minute."

I direct him to the bookshelf when he gets to my room. "Can you see if anything slipped into the gap there?"

"Did you drop a book?" he says. I don't answer.

"Move back," he says, trying to pull the shelf away. It doesn't budge immediately. He tries again and the shelf moves an inch.

"Damn it."

"It's all right," I say. "Never mind."

But Louis is stubborn. After a few minutes, he pulls the shelf far enough away from the wall to fit his arm through the gap.

He pulls out a brown planner covered in dust bunnies. A planner with a leather cover, thick with inserts.

Louis hands it to me. I brush away the thick film of dust and open it. Out falls a university ID. Louis bends to pick it up. The name on the ID is Meryl Solomon.

We stare at it as if it could cause an explosion.

Is Meryl here?

"Oh my God, Louis," I say.

But the college girl smiling from the square of plastic has flesh on her bones, round cheeks, a big smile. Health. Not the near-skeleton in the freezer.

"Is that her?" I ask.

"I don't know," he says. "I can hardly remember her face now." He reads the name of the school. "This university is not far from here."

"Really?"

We sit together in miserable silence.

"Can I see?" Louis asks, and I am more than glad to hand the planner to him.

6

Louis pores over the contents of the planner during dinner. The tables have turned—now I'm the one scarfing down rice and fish while Louis ignores his plate.

"You need to eat something," I say, echoing his words for me earlier. How far away that beef stew seemed now, pre-chest freezer. Pre-dead girl.

From the various slots in the planner, we uncovered a purple pen, a torn ticket stub to a play at the university, a folded piece of paper with equations marked "Fundamental Accounting", a flyer for a jeans sale ("UP TO 75% OFF!"), and small cardboard cards covered in calligraphy script. *Sweetness. Elegance. Fuck.*

Louis turns the pages of the planner, every now and then turning to me and pointing at something the girl has written. We look at her calendar. It is March. *Final group paper due.*

She has encircled a date in April. *Solo trip—can't wait to see you Vigan!!! Can't wait to get OUT of here.*

She is supposed to enter her senior year in college by June. She has notes up to that month, sweet June that she never saw. *Online pre-enlistment. Comm 180.*

I suddenly find it hard to breathe.

"This poor girl," Louis says.

"I hope it's not her," I say. "The one in the freezer. I hope it's not Meryl." But that would mean an anonymous corpse and a potential witness to the crime.

We come upon a page filled with names and phone numbers, but Louis skips ahead, probably planning to deal with that later.

"Look at this," Louis says.

The page shows a photo of people sitting in a circle. Cut from a magazine, taped on the page.

Meryl used black ink for her notes and wrote in beautiful cursive.

- Hi I'm Meryl, and I'm overweight.
- Hi Meryl!
- Really, it's okay, I don't even know why we need to make a big deal out of this.

The next page is an Alice in Wonderland collage, blonde Alice in a blue dress with a mushroom umbrella. The Cheshire cat. Lace. Glitter. Pink swatches. We turn the page.

I don't want to go home, to be honest. I'd avoid it if I could. This is all they see: one hundred and seventy pounds. I am doing well in my studies, thank you for not asking, and yes this dress doesn't fit me anymore. Alice ate the Eat Me Cake, the foolish slut.

I was 120 pounds when I entered college. I bought bigger jeans, upped my shirt size. It didn't feel like a big deal. I was enjoying myself. But one time I came home and my mother looked at me and said, "You are so fat," with such incredulity and such disgust that every spoonful I consumed felt like sin.

The next page shows another magazine cutout, a photo of a gray-haired couple smiling at the camera. *We'll love you if you are exactly this size!* the caption reads.

There was a time when my cousins and I went out and had a spa day. A cousin of mine apparently saw the (petite) masseuse roll her eyes while kneading my shoulders. My cousin said, she's too big for you, isn't she? And they all laughed and of course I had to laugh because I had to be a good sport, I can't be fat AND sensitive, oh no, because I did this to myself, didn't I? Then we had dinner and I ended up paying for their food. I don't know why I do this to myself.

I have been called a whale. I have been asked in jest if I were pregnant, and why the gestation period was so long. Someone in class I didn't even know very well asked me to come over, gestured "wide" with her arms, and asked, "What the hell happened?"

I have more stories like this. Maybe you'd like to sit down.

I hate: pencil skirts, scuba gear, sleeveless tops, family reunions, college mixers, a gathering of any kind that involves people looking you up and down and passing judgment on you even before you open your mouth, i.e. she is fat, therefore she is: lazy, undisciplined, greedy, has thunder thighs that will rip apart the dress she's wearing. Any. Second. Now.

The funny thing is I go on a diet, I drink lots of water, and my classmates eat pizza and burgers and drink soda every day yet they remain reed-thin while I am this. And the world looks at us, points at me and says I eat like a monster. I did not create this body—it was given to me.

I am also a pretty decent artist, but who the fuck cares.

There is a pastel drawing of a little girl with her arms spread wide. Over her is a rainbow, and over the rainbow is an arc of words that read, *Fuck your heart, appearance is everything.*

Appearance is everything.

Immediately following this is a list of food and measurements, like this:

Oatmeal—40 g—150 cal.
Coffee—240 g—5 cal.
Adobo chicken—227 g—300 cal.
Mixed fruit—140 g—59 cal.

Nilaga—?—210? cal.

Resistance training—30 min.—143 cal. burned

This goes on for three or so pages.

Then:

I am doing my best. I really am, but I lose the weight and then gain it right back.

I want to do this for myself. I think, This is for my health (though I am healthy! I am!), but I feel like I am doing this to lord it over my mother, to wipe the smirk off my cousin's face, to answer the girl who had the audacity to ask me, What the hell happened? This is what happened, bitch.

But I fail. I fail and I fail and I fail.

I hear the girls talking about fasting but I can't do it. I want to. It's the fastest way to make myself disappear.

Why can't I do this? Why can't I just slice off this flab and get on with my life?

I feel the urge to jump on a bus, any bus, to anywhere, and just go away and never come back.

Can we just stop making me feel like shit already? Can we do that?

I want to love myself, but it appears that I am not allowed to.

You are so fat, you are so worthless, you take up the space meant for better, more disciplined people, WHY DO YOU EVEN BOTHER, MERYL?

The very last entry is dated January 1, the New Year, and reads: *I am so tired of this body.*

I miss pacing. I miss putting my hands in my pocket and striding from one end of the room to another, because I can, because I want to, because I am frustrated and anxious and movement helps ease this sinking feeling.

I push myself away from the table and wheel out of the dining room, through the living room, and out the door onto the front porch. There is a soft breeze. I wonder where the breeze is coming from. Is there a sea nearby? The street we are on is narrow and quiet and sad, the sea's antithesis.

I think of everything other than Meryl and her last words, but of course every thought circles back to her.

I hear the door open behind me. Louis steps out to sit on the porch ledge.

"It's probably the most harrowing thing I've read in my life," I say.

Louis looks past the gate, at the other houses. "If that was her in the chest freezer," he says, "it looks like she was starved to death."

"She sounded like she *wanted* to starve to death." I shake my head. "It's a horrible fixation."

"Why was she here?" Louis says. "What was her connection to you and me?"

To Louis and Jonah, you mean, I think.

I think about the planner, where we found it. I wheel across the porch toward my bedroom window. I peer inside. The low bookshelf. The bed, the bedroom door beyond. It is a bungalow, after all. The window is large. It is a short drop.

"She was trying to get out of the window," I say. "Someone trapped her in the bedroom, blocking the doorway. She hoisted herself up onto the bookshelf to open the window and her planner fell into the gap."

And then what? She wasn't able to open the windows fast enough. Someone wrapped their arms around her and pulled her back into the house. I imagine her kicking, scratching, her sneakers hitting the books, the books falling to the floor.

We go to my room. We look at the hardwood floor. We can see scratches, but we don't know how long they have been there. Last night, last month, years ago?

"But why?" Louis asks.

Why would she go here? Why would anyone want to keep her here?

Why do we need to care?

"Louis," I say, "let's not get involved in this."

Louis sighs and sits on the edge of the bed. "We keep the body a secret," he says. He says it deadpan; I can't tell if he's judging me.

"Yes."

"And the planner?"

"We bury it. Burn it."

"And then what?"

And then—

I don't answer.

"And then we wait for you to get better," says Louis. "And while we wait, there is the danger of the police or Meryl's family finding out where she was last seen."

"She's probably been missing since early this year," I say, "and yet her body's still here."

Just a few days ago, a young woman approached the gate and asked if Meryl was in this house.

Louis doesn't bring it up. "All right. You get better. We leave this city, go someplace else. With bodies and identities that may be guilty of a crime."

I don't say anything. Then: "Let's take the body out of the freezer and bury it."

"At the risk of our neighbors seeing something?"

"What neighbors?" I scoff.

"You're right. It's a quiet street. But are you a hundred percent sure there's no nocturnal teenager looking out of his window into our backyard right now?"

"There's the spell," I say.

Louis falls silent for a moment. "Well," he says. He stands up, begins to pace. I wish I could do the same. "It's flimsy. It won't hold up for long. And it's only meant to keep uninvited people out, not make the house invisible."

"We find another body to switch to," I say.

He stops walking. "I told you," he says. "We can't do this again. You saw what happened to—"

I know. I know. But—

"We were able to perfectly make the switch," I say, and almost instantly feel the throb of pain in my right leg, my ruined knee, the throb increasing in magnitude, crushing like a vise.

Louis runs out and comes back with opioids and a glass of water.

"What's the endgame here, Louis?" I ask, minutes later. I imagine myself at sea, I imagine the pain as a series of waves, ebbing, leaving.

"I'm sorry," Louis says, and I am instantly angry at him for ignoring my question. "I didn't mean to fight. I will bury the planner in the garden tomorrow. That should be easy enough. My first thought really was to move the body, but I can't—" He pauses. "I don't want to touch her."

The anger dissipates. I think of him, the real him, in our previous life, five years older and brighter, kinder, more compassionate, than my own father. I remember the forbidden books he smuggled into the estate so I could have something more worthwhile to read, some world more worthwhile to visit. Something to aspire to. His stories and the books he brought created something that wasn't there before—a want—and I still can't decide if this first act of rebellion against our fathers is a good thing or a bad thing. If it was worth it.

"I hope they abandon the search soon," Louis is saying now. "I checked online, there is a small article about a missing student named Meryl Solomon. There is an ongoing search. There are social network groups talking about her and her last whereabouts but they all seem stumped."

Look at what has happened to us.

"What's the endgame here?" I ask again.

He doesn't reply.

"You plan to stay in these bodies until we die?" I say.

"Do you have a better plan?"

I am so surprised by his rage that I am rendered mute.

"If I can give you my right leg I would," Louis says, "but I can't. These are the cards we were dealt."

I give myself a pep talk every morning: you are injured but you are away from the estate, you are with your cousin who is kind enough to take care of you, you have a chance to live a new life. You should be grateful, you should be grateful, you should be grateful.

But I have listened to the doctors, I have read the literature. I should be able to use crutches along with the brace to move about in the first six weeks post-surgery ("early weight-bearing is encouraged") but the pain is incredible. Even my left leg can't seem to carry me. Sometimes I can't feel anything below my right knee. I know—I am sure—that there will be more surgeries down the road, years of rehabilitation, recurrent dislocations, chronic pain, dependence on drugs, and a brace I have to wear my whole life. If Meryl was still alive I would tell her, *Rejoice in your life, rejoice in your beautiful, healthy body, in your lack of hurt.* I would tell her family and her detractors that they are fools, that they have marred a crystal-clear happiness. I mourn Meryl. And I mourn the boy who once climbed a tree, fell from its branches, and rebounded just a week later, ready to play again. I mourn my previous body now probably locked up in a morgue somewhere, about to head to an unmarked mass grave. It was disease-free, resilient, and strong. It was not in pain. Such a waste, I think now, but: *you should be grateful, you should be grateful, you should be grateful.*

"I don't want to be stuck in this body," I say, and I am surprised by the hitch in my breath, the tears on my cheeks. My ruined knee throbs. I cover my face with my right hand. I want to be left alone, I don't want to be touched, but when Louis leans forward and embraces me, I don't push him away.

The sad thing about pain is that you can't share it or pass it on, no matter how willing the next person is. No one can take agony away from you, no matter how many times the people you love tell you, I know exactly how you feel. You know they really don't. You suffer alone, in the end.

8

ouis digs a hole near the porch the next morning, drops the planner in, and covers it carefully with a layer of soil and fertilizer. He stands up. I watch him look through the potted plants beneath the bougainvillea bushes and pull out a clay pot carrying a pale yellow chrysanthemum plant. He brings this to the hole. He takes the flower along with its roots out of the pot and places the plant into the soil. There are other flowers lining the porch—geraniums, peonies—but the chrysanthemum stands out, its petals pale against the lush pinks and purples. I don't see it from my bedroom window, but when I roll out onto the porch and lean forward, it stares back at me like an infected eye.

The TV in the living room has been largely ignored ever since we got here, but Louis watches the news now every night. I know what he is waiting for. I don't listen, choosing, as always, to stay in my room or out on the porch with a book until I get sleepy.

For a few days, we almost—almost—make ourselves believe there is no dead body in the basement.

It is Thursday, three days since the planner was buried. Since it is drizzling, I decide to go to my room instead of out on the porch. "What are you reading today," Louis asks idly, sinking into his usual spot on the sofa in front of the TV, but I never get to answer because the evening news has begun and up on the screen is Meryl's big smile.

The decomposing body believed to be that of Meryl Angela Solomon, an 18-year-old college student reported missing last January, was found by police in an abandoned building on university grounds.

Louis freezes for a second, then sits up, and leans forward, as though a closer look at the screen will help him understand the story better. I wheel myself around the sofa.

There are shots of a dark one-story building surrounded by tall grass; policemen walking, windows, cobwebs, graffiti on stone walls.

Solomon's body was found wearing a white shirt and jeans. A backpack filled with her belongings, including several of her IDs and a silver necklace, was also found with the body.

Shots of a purple backpack, covered in grime. Her IDs on a table. Some books. A silver necklace with a sapphire teardrop pendant. A body bag on a gurney.

Police began an on-site investigation following reports of a foul smell emanating from the old Fine Arts building. The building has not been used for five years and is generally avoided by students as it sits on a remote, unlit field.

The building has been the site of on-campus crime in the past.

Due to the body's advanced decomposition, investigators relied on the contents of the backpack to identify the body. Forensic analysis will follow but investigators admit identification might be difficult.

Cause of death is still unknown.

Solomon's family expressed doubt about the identity of the body, but agreed that the backpack and its contents belonged to the 18-year-old.

A middle-aged woman with curly hair and beads of sweat on her forehead wipes her eyes but continues to cry in front of the camera. Her eyes are pink and swollen. Meryl's mother. *"The necklace was a gift from Meryl's grandmother. She can't wear it because she says it makes her skin itch, but she always brings it with her."*

Solomon was due to start her last year at the university's School of Economics in June.

Louis and I, dumbfounded, stare at the TV as the anchor moves on to another news item.

"If that's Meryl," I say, "then who is—"

Who is that girl in the freezer?

Louis looks at me. "You know what this means, right?"

"What?"

"We're safe," he says.

Safe. Now there's a word. But he is right. No one will come looking for Meryl in this house now, because Meryl has been found.

"But there's still a body in the freezer," I say.

"I know," he says. "I'll keep an eye out for any news about missing persons."

After a moment, Louis says, "I still think it's Meryl, though. The one downstairs."

"Did we cover up our own crime?" I say. We kill a girl in the basement, and to stop people from looking our way, we plant a fake body with genuine Meryl articles far, far away from the actual scene of the crime.

Louis massages his eyes with his thumb and forefinger.

"Who *are* we?" I say. But who can answer?

9

We can answer, but there is no one and nothing left to investigate other than the objects the brothers have left behind. Before we have found the planner I have rummaged through Jonah's drawers and cabinet. Now I survey the things I found. An old wallet. A box of assorted business cards. Receipts, folded and forgotten, some already frayed and yellowing. A set of keys that don't open any of the rooms in the house. An expanding plastic folder filled with handouts, brochures, and IDs from several conventions. *Exploring IT @ the SMX Convention Center. Information, People, Tech. International Conference on Web Information Systems. International Conference on Advances in Information Technology.* A strange 3 x 5 index card that says *Big business is a sociopath—manipulative, remorseless, grandiose, entitled* on one side and *I love the way you think* (written by another hand) on the other. A photo collage from a company Christmas party, more than two years old. Jonah stares straight at the camera, his arms around some friends. Head canted at an angle, a smile like he knows something. I face the mirror in the cabinet and try to mimic the pose, the glint in the eye. I can't do it. I look terrified of myself.

I am in the middle of unfolding the bigger brochures and convention maps when Louis checks in on me.

"What in the world are you doing?"

I pause, my lap covered with glossy photos of buildings.

"Investigating," I say.

Louis sits on the edge of the bed and looks through the folder. I hear paper rustle as he rifles quickly through a handbook. "We taught at the University," he says.

I stop reading. "What?"

"I found a syllabus on his computer. My computer. Louis's computer." He shakes his head, trying to get his story straight. "Louis and Jonah taught at the university for a semester last year, and for a couple of months the year before that. We were invited by a former professor to teach a course or two. Business units."

"Meryl was a student of ours?"

"She's an Econ major. It's possible."

"I don't know how that fits in her story."

Louis sighs. "I don't know either. But I found something else. An itinerary receipt." I must have looked confused because Louis elaborates. "An electronic plane ticket. I'm basing the travel itinerary on his social networks and his email. We flew to Cebu on January 16 to attend a friend's wedding then took a ferry to Bohol to give talks at an IT seminar. We were out of this city for weeks. Our return ticket was dated February 1. It can be an alibi."

"If we can figure out when Meryl actually died," I say. "She has been missing since January. We could have killed her and flew out of the city on the same day."

"Remember her entries," Louis says. "She mentioned her weight. That near-skeleton in the freezer is nowhere near a hundred and seventy pounds."

"We locked her up?" I shake my head. I'm too confused. Too many parts of the puzzle are missing.

I can forget the body in the freezer for hours at a time, but when I remember her, I remember her with the jolt of a terrifying dream you think you have forgotten, and I feel myself falling.

I used to be able to sleep in absolute darkness, but since Louis discovered Meryl, I have asked Louis to leave the porch light on so I can have light coming in through my bedroom window. This soon proves to be a mistake. That night—I don't know if this happens in a dream or in real life—I see a girl's silhouette pass by from the corner of the house to the front door. The shadow walks on the porch right in front of my window and the slice of darkness falling on my face wakes me up so abruptly I almost fall off the bed.

It is just a flicker, gone in a moment. I think, *I am seeing things.* I try to go back to sleep, turning my head the other way, even though the square of light falls across my bed and on the opposite wall.

It happens again. I see the dark shape on the wall. I see the shape of the medium-length hair, the shoulders. The shadow doesn't move this time. It stays there, facing my window.

I am terrified, but I spare a glance to my right. There is a shadow standing outside my bedroom window. I turn away again and shut my eyes. I want to call Louis's attention, but there is no phone in my room and the only way to get his attention is to scream. I am trapped. Can't sit up, can't walk out to get help, can't run. Can't even lie on my side to banish the shadow from my field of vision. It lingers in the periphery. I am helpless. I will the shadow away. It remains there for what seems like hours.

I am sorry. I am so sorry.

Finally, I say, "Is that you, Meryl?" and I feel a hand shaking me and light fills my eyes, as sudden and as brutal as a car crash.

Louis is in my room and the bedroom light is on. "I was just getting water," he says. "You were moaning. I thought you needed your pain medication. Bad dream?"

Bad dream. My shirt is soaked with sweat. Louis hands me a new shirt and leaves after making sure I am not in pain. I am not. It is just a bad dream.

I can't sleep after that.

"You look like hell," Louis says over breakfast.

There is fried rice, sausage, and eggs on the table between us but neither of us eat. Louis eventually lifts his mug and takes a sip of coffee.

"Do you dream about her?" I ask, and then realize how vague my question is. "I mean, Meryl. Do you dream about her?"

"Last night I dreamt I was in the basement, sitting next to the chest freezer," Louis replies. "She was standing in one corner of the basement. I can't see her directly but I know she's there. Still, for some reason, I talked to the chest freezer. I can't remember what I said."

"I wish we could ask her what really happened," I say.

We fall silent. Louis sips his coffee. I tug on a thread of thought that's been bothering me for days.

"Where are our parents?" I ask.

Louis looks up, surprised. "You've asked me this at the hospital. Don't you remember?"

There are a lot of things I don't remember. I shake my head.

"They're dead," Louis says. "But we seem to have relatives abroad. While you were in surgery, I received a call from Canada. A woman, maybe an aunt of ours. She was screaming in my ear. It took thirty minutes to placate her."

"What did you find in your room?"

Louis seems a bit confused by the topic change, but he answers. "I found the same convention packets. Passport. Driver's license. Voter's ID. Business cards. Our business's business cards, actually."

"I also found business cards from other contacts and they all look old," I say. "Except for a set of keys, I only found old things. An old wallet. Old receipts. An old picture. The kind of things you leave behind. There is no passport, which is strange because both brothers have clearly been abroad. Nothing current or important. There's the closet full of clothes, but not a lot of clothes, when you think about it. Most of the shirts I've worn smell like mothballs."

Louis puts down his mug. "What are you thinking?"

I'm thinking of the cleaning lady, how she held Louis's hands and told him how kind he was to take care of his brother. "I'm thinking," I say, "that Jonah doesn't live here. He used to; one of the rooms was clearly his. Maybe the brothers shared the house while still in college, and Jonah eventually moved out."

"Makes sense," Louis says. "I only went to the address on Louis's driver's license and just assumed that Jonah lived here, too."

"So, this is your house," I say. *And the body in the basement is yours.*

"And out there is a house with all of your belongings," says Louis. "Evidence we haven't inspected yet."

We can't find Jonah's physical address and the keys offer no clues. Jonah didn't write it down on a page for his brother. It is not in Louis's emails, or in his phone. But really, why should it be? Nobody sends out letters anymore. They have the Internet. And if Louis has a package to send, he can just drive out and meet up with his brother.

"I never knew your address outside the estate," I say. We're both hunched over Louis's laptop, though we both know there's nothing to see there.

"You have no reason to," Louis says.

That's right.

"Do you think Louis is capable of murder?" I ask. "From what you've learned about him?"

Louis shrugged. "What do we know? He has this house and he likes to garden and doesn't seem to like to mingle with the neighbors. He doesn't have a lot of friends, or the friends he does have know enough to leave him alone, even after a serious accident. He seems like a decent enough guy. He's very proper in his emails. He pays his bills on time. It's hard to gauge a person's character based on what he does online, and that's the bulk of what we have, really. I can't judge him based on his search history. Do you remember the online searches we made at the estate? If your mother ever saw what we—"

52

He starts to smile but then he catches himself. He clears his throat. "I'm sorry. We shouldn't talk about it."

"Do you think Jonah is capable of murder?" I ask, and Louis sighs.

"I never," he says, "in all of my years believed we were capable of murder."

Yes. "And yet here we are," I say.

10

The girl in the costume is back. I haven't seen her for days. The pink fairy wings are gone, and now she is wearing a white dress and a blue-and-gold falcon mask. She stands there on the other side of the street, doing a little dance. I feel the urge to wave at her, but the front door opens—Louis out to do some gardening—and she runs away.

It has rained that night so the morning breeze is cool, as if it were January. Louis has opened my bedroom window before stepping out. I turn my face to the light wind and call out to Louis.

"Yes?" he says.

"Did you see that girl?" I ask.

"What girl?"

"The little girl? Across the street? She was wearing a mask."

"No, I didn't see her."

She was the twins' age, I want to say.

"Neighbor's kid," Louis says, and begins watering the plants.

I see her first. An hour has passed and Louis is busy weeding the flowers, his back to the gate, when I hear the whir of a bicycle going down the street. The girl is wearing a skirt over leggings, a black shirt, a leather bag slung across her chest. She could have been any other girl, if not for the magenta hair.

A moment later, her bike tilts to the ground and she is falling. She must have bounced on a pothole, a tiny hump. I can't see a thing, except for her legs under the wheels. She has screamed before the spill—a loud, crisp *Ah!*—and now she is groaning, trying to push herself up. She starts to cry. She produces a soft sound like that of an abandoned kitten.

Louis runs to the gate when he hears her scream. He wraps his fingers around the gate's bars. *Don't let her in,* I implore him in my head. *Don't talk to her.*

Then Louis does the one thing he has never done ever since helping me into this house: he opens the gate and steps out.

Louis bends over the girl, hands on his knees, and talks to her. The girl stops crying long enough to raise her head and reply. He offers his hands and helps her up. She's nearly as tall as Louis. She wobbles on her feet. They look down at the same time, presumably at her torn leggings, the wounds on her legs.

Louis lets her hold his arm. He looks up, sees me through the bedroom window. I shake my head—*Don't. Let. Her. In.*— even though I already know what he is going to do.

He lets her in.

He swings the gate as wide as it would go and tells her something. An invitation. A permission. The magenta-haired girl hesitates for a second, looking at the gate, probably remembering the first time she was there.

She steps across the perimeter—I see her exhale; she has held her breath before stepping through—and walks down the driveway with her head bowed. She sits on the porch steps. Louis rights the bicycle and wheels it into the front yard.

I watch all this with growing horror. When the girl glances over her shoulder, I duck and wheel away from the window like a criminal.

I hear them outside my door. They're in the living room. "I'm sorry to put you out like this," the girl says. "Thanks for helping." The last word dissolves into sobs. "I'm so sorry."

"It's all right," Louis says. "My name is Louis."

"Ivy," the girl says, her voice shaking.

"Why don't you sit here, Ivy?" Louis says. "I'll be back with the first-aid kit and a glass of water."

I have been hoping to catch Louis mid-stride, but by the time I open the door and wheel out, he is already in the kitchen, and I'm left facing the girl, sitting on one of the armchairs and staring into space.

She turns to me and her shoulders jerk in surprise. I see her glance quickly at my bound leg. "Oh," she says. "Hello."

"Hi," I say.

Louis sweeps in at that moment, carrying the kit and a glass of water. He hands the water to Ivy.

"This is my brother, Jonah," he says.

"Hi," Ivy says.

"Hi," I say again, like we're a broken record. "Listen, I need to talk to my brother for a minute."

Louis joins me in the room. "What?" he whispers after closing the door.

"What do you mean 'what'?" I point to the living room. "What are you doing?"

"You can't expect me to just leave her on the ground," he says. "She could hardly walk."

"But she *knows* Meryl. Why would you even invite her inside?"

Louis shakes his head and walks out to tend to his new patient.

When I leave my room, Ivy is taping down the gauze Louis holds in place on the large wound on her knee. Her leggings are on the floor. Her left elbow is bright with topical antiseptic.

"Damn," Ivy says, sniffling. "Those were new leggings." She chuckles weakly.

Louis says she can't ride back on the bicycle again and offers to call her a cab. Ivy and I sit in awkward silence as Louis talks on the phone. She looks antsy and nervous.

"So," I say, "do you live in the area?"

She smiles. "No." The smile disappears and her lower lip trembles. She wipes her eyes. "Have you heard about the college girl who was found dead on-campus a few days ago?"

Louis is back in the room with us. "The cab will be here in twenty minutes," he says.

Silence. I try to thaw the ice that has formed in my chest. "You were talking about the Solomon girl," I prompt Ivy. Louis glances at me and looks away in a blink of an eye. "Meryl?"

Ivy doesn't know who we are. She doesn't know that Meryl was probably one of our former students.

Doesn't know that Meryl's real body is here with us.

"She's a friend of mine," Ivy says. "We're roommates. The day before she failed to come home to the boarding house, I dropped her on this street."

"Oh my God," Louis says, which is probably the more appropriate thing to do, instead of steeling myself on my chair, bracing for impact.

"When was that?" Louis asks.

"January 16," Ivy says, wiping away an errant teardrop. "It was a Wednesday. I was in Meycauayan for my brother's birthday Tuesday night, and he lent me his car so I could just drive to campus instead of taking the bus. I didn't have class, so I picked up Meryl after hers and we had lunch. Then she asked me to drop her here, just at the intersection. She said she just needs to take photos for a project. I offered to come with her, but she said she wanted to do it alone. She seemed a bit pissed off at me for insisting so much. That reaction got me riled up as well—I was just being nice—so I left and I never saw her again."

"And you don't know where she went?"

Ivy shakes her head. "I've been biking around here ever since they found the body." Her voice trembles at the last word. "I was wondering if there were any shops here, anything colorful that she could photograph, but there was only a playground, residential blocks. I did bring a picture of hers so I can show it to people here and ask if any of them saw her, but no one did." She shrugs, lowers her voice, as though she's talking to herself. "And anyway, I don't remember her bringing her DSLR."

"They didn't find a camera in her bag," I say.

"Yes, so maybe she lied to me." She looks at her hands.

"Have you told the police about this?" Louis asks.

She nods. "I was among the first to be interviewed. But there were conflicting reports. I remember letting her off here at around 2 pm. But some classmates of hers claimed they saw her at around the same time at Trudy's, which is a small café nearby. I don't know. Maybe I got the time wrong. Maybe her classmates saw someone else. Maybe after I left her here, she took a cab and went to have coffee on her own. No one is sure, so I guess the police just noted it down and went on their way."

"I'm sorry about your friend," Louis says.

Ivy nods and claws open her sling bag. "The week she was identified, I went through her things. It's probably a bad thing, but her parents are coming over and Meryl might be keeping something she didn't want her folks to see." She smiles and sniffs. "Friends, you know? You need to have a good friend around after you go so she can clear your search history."

She puts five glossy prints on the coffee table. My heart drops.

"I didn't know." Ivy wipes her eyes. "I didn't know she felt this way. She is beautiful. She has no idea. She is beautiful and I should have told her."

They are blown-up high-resolution prints of pages from Meryl's planner. At least two are larger recreations of her collages. Her planner is the sketchbook of ideas and these are the artwork you can frame and display. Alice in Meryl's sad wonderland, her kingdom of lace. *Alice ate the Eat Me Cake, the foolish slut.*

Ivy asks if she can have a smoke while waiting for her cab so I accompany her on the porch while Louis tidies up inside.

Small talk. I ask her about her major. "Journalism," she says. She is sitting on the porch step, blowing smoke up to the sky, a protective arm across the sling bag she hugs to her chest.

"You want to be a reporter?"

She chuckles. "You can work in media or PR. At the end of journalism school, the students will either be the reporters or the source of the story."

"And who do you think you would be?"

"Neither. I'd probably just work in a call center receiving daily abuse from American clients."

She has been crying constantly ever since her bicycle fell. Maybe even long before. "You and Meryl were close," I say.

She goes still and nods. The yellow chrysanthemum moves in the light breeze, nodding with her.

"The news says they were only able to identify the body based on the bag and its contents," I say.

"I have this fantasy," Ivy says, "that the girl they found in the building was someone else. A thief. Just a stranger who happened to have Meryl's stuff, and Meryl is somewhere else, alive and enjoying an early summer vacation." She shrugs. "My mother says a mother's intuition is never wrong. I spoke to Meryl's mother on the phone. You know what she said?"

She waits for me to shake my head. I shake my head.

"She says it's horrible but she knows in her heart that her daughter is already dead."

I feel the planner throbbing like a heart beneath the earth. I remember my dream and the shadow on the wall.

Ivy wipes her eyes. "You can't argue with that."

"I'm so sorry," I say.

"I should have told her," Ivy says. I remember the glossy prints hitting the coffee table with a splat.

"You shouldn't blame yourself," I say.

"No, I—" Ivy sighs and smiles at me. She shakes her head.

Louis helps Ivy with her bike when the cab arrives. "Thank you for all your help," she says. "I promise to come back with some cake."

"Come back any time," Louis says. "Even without the cake."

At that point I realize why Louis let her in, why he's inviting her back. What better way to find out new developments about the case than through the victim's adamant friend? This way, we know what they know.

11

vy comes back after three days, carrying not only a box of cake, but also a covered Pyrex bowl filled with *pancit*. "I wasn't sure if you like sweets so I brought something savory," she explains. Louis, of course, lets her in once again, and takes out three plates and three forks, her invitation to stay.

In those three days, news about Meryl centered mostly on the university's beefed-up security, CCTVs in the lobbies, and additional guards in civilian clothes carrying flashlights and *arnis* sticks. The University President implores students to avoid walking alone, especially at night.

I let Louis take care of the small talk. They talk about her fall, how her wounds are starting to scab. I help him when the conversation veers away from Ivy and into our general direction.

"So, you live here together?" she asks.

"No," Louis says, glancing at me. "This is just a temporary arrangement."

I tap my knee immobilizer when I see her frown in confusion. Ivy presses her lips together and lifts her chin—*Oh*—and lapses into a heavy, awkward silence.

"So, what are you up to now?" Louis asks as she burrows further into her slice of cake. She will be the only one touching that cake. After she leaves, Louis will return the rest to the box and dump it in the trash.

She shrugs. "Exams. Papers."

"Life goes on?" Louis says, with surprising tenderness.

Ivy nods. After a moment, she lifts her sling bag from the floor and takes out a laptop. She boots it up. She has Van Gogh's *Blossoming Almond Tree* as wallpaper.

"I've been interviewing people about Meryl," she says as she scrolls through her files. "I plan to make a video about her and the case. Can I show this to you? Maybe you can give me some comments."

It's like manna from heaven. We try not to look too eager when we say yes.

Ivy warns us that it is a partial rough cut before playing the video.

Onscreen appears a girl of Ivy's age, her hair curled at the ends. She is wearing a maroon sash with the word, "Usher". She helps people find their seats in an auditorium, probably the university auditorium. Cut to the same girl posing with fellow ushers at a lobby. She makes a V with her forefinger and middle finger and flashes a smile at the camera. Cut to the same girl in a corridor with other college students. She is wearing a dress. "Her?" she says, and laughs. "I wouldn't invite her to the party. She'll go insane. She's like the Fox News of people."

"There's supposed to be a VO over all that," Ivy tells us. "'Just three months after the death of—'"

I look at the girl again.

"Who is she?" Louis asks.

"Mona. She's also an Econ major, like Meryl, but from a lower batch." She takes a sip of water. "She was found dead in December, before the break. She jumped from the topmost floor of the Engineering building."

"That's horrible. Do they know why?"

Ivy shakes her head. "No letter. I don't really know her, but her classmates say Mona looked pretty depressed the week before she jumped. A news story or two in the papers mentioned her, you know, for background." Ivy looks at the screen. "She's popular, but girls hate her. You know what I mean? She has this reputation of being loose. Sleeping around. Flirting with other girls' boyfriends. Meryl thinks she must have been on drugs. She told me that one time, during Econ, Mona suddenly started screaming and left the room in tears."

"She and Meryl were friends?" Louis asks.

Ivy snorts. "Meryl hated her."

Fade to black. White words on black: *Meryl.*

Fade in to—

Joanne, BS Economics, petite girl with hair dyed brown: "She's a co-applicant of mine to the Econ Circle, but she didn't go through with her application."

The students were interviewed separately, Ivy just cutting from one talking head to another. The student's name and major appear at the bottom of the screen.

Jeffrey, BA Journalism, lanky guy with rimless glasses: (*rubs his chin*) "I can't remember if it's PE or Math."

Kayla, BS Business Administration, tall girl with a face

64

scrubbed clean, her unlined pale lips fading into her skin: "I definitely remember. I was a grumpy SA. I snapped at her when she brought me an incomplete form for enrollment and she burst into tears right at the counter. *(listens to Ivy, who is unintelligible behind the camera)* I know! *(laughs, covers her face)* It's a horrible 'How did you meet her' story. I apologized, of course. I felt guilty the entire semester."

Leslie, BS Business Administration, round face, long wavy hair that keeps blowing into her eyes, blue eyeshadow: "We were classmates in several Econ majors. My electives, you know? Elements of Mathematical Economics, exciting subjects like that." *(laughs)*

Arman, BS Economics, short guy with close-cropped hair: "She was my seatmate at Freshman Orientation. I remember because when the host asked us to dance in place, she looked at me and we were like, 'Are you kidding me right now?'" *(Ivy: "Did you dance?")* "I'd rather not say." *(They laugh.)*

Joanne: "Sweet—"

Jeffrey: "Very smart—"

Kayla: "—just talented and—"

Leslie: "—she drew this funny caricature in like ten seconds—"

Arman: "—and I asked her, "What the hell are you doing studying Economics?""

Fade to black. White words on black: *Last encounter.*

Joanne: "I don't remember. Isn't that awful? I think I asked her if she had copies of the 109 readings."

Jeffrey: "We were supposed to go drinking. With you! *(points to somewhere off-camera; Ivy says, "Yes")* But she flaked out, and we ended up drinking with the other guys. That was the last time I spoke to her."

Kayla: "She asked me if I had a book for her BA class. I gave her an earlier edition. That book was found in the—" *(gestures with her hands)* "— you know. In the bag. With the—" *(Ivy says, "Yeah", and Kayla drops her hands and sighs)* "Yes."

Leslie: "She was my partner, for a paper. For Money & Banking. I invited her to my house so we could talk about it—also hey, free *merienda* from my mother—but she never showed up." *(listens to Ivy)* "I live with my family, yes. In Ortigas. That was in mid-January, then she was reported missing and I just felt terrible because I was so annoyed with her for missing our meeting."

Arman: "She was a classmate of mine in Quanti. We talked a bit before class, but I didn't see her after and that's the last time I was able to speak to her."

Leslie: "She was quieter, I suppose. I don't know. I didn't notice anything alarming, really."

Kayla: *(thinks)* "No. I don't—She seemed like herself."

Joanne: "A package for her arrived at the department."

Arman: "It was in a box, like the size of a book." *(gestures)*

Jeffrey: "It was addressed to her. Probably hand-carried. Nobody knows how long it's been in the Inbox tray."

Kayla: "Package?"

Leslie: "I didn't know about a package. She never mentioned it."

Jeffrey: "It's probably been there a while. Remember that time I had an Incomplete because our dick of a professor didn't see my paper in his pigeonhole? I wouldn't be surprised if that package has been in there since the last curriculum change."

Joanne: "The Department Secretary discovered it after the Christmas break and gave it to her."

Arman: "Joanne, Jeff, some other batchmates. We were all pestering *Ate* Malou for the projector."

Joanne: "She didn't open it at the office but I did ask her about it the next day. She seemed flustered. Like she was lying but couldn't get the facts straight." *(Ivy asks something.)* "A Moleskine, gift from an uncle. It *was* the size of a notebook, but I don't know. She seemed nervous about it."

Arman: "No, I never asked."

Jeffrey: "Did she tell you about it?" *(Ivy replies.)* "See, and you practically live with her."

Arman: "It's probably nothing."

Joanne: "You know how, when you desperately want the answer to something, your brain just snags on the stupidest details? I was thinking what was different about her before she went missing, and that package is what I remembered." *(Ivy says, "I do remember her *unintelligible* I even told her, "You're so grumpy nowadays".)*

Leslie: "Do you think it's really her, though? The one in FA?" *(Ivy replies.)*

Kayla: "I can't imagine what her family's going through." *(Ivy says, "Sometimes you wonder if it's better to know for sure, instead of ending up with what we got, you know, a body no one can positively identify.")*

Joanne: *(crying and sniffing; wipes her eyes with her fingers)* "Sorry, Ivy."

12

The video ends. Louis and I stare at Ivy. She is crying as well, like Joanne, BS Economics.

"Thank you," Louis says, "for letting us see it."

She takes a deep breath and smiles. "Thanks for watching." She shuts down the laptop and returns it to her bag. "It still looks shitty."

"They mentioned a package?" I say. Louis gives me a sharp look. I frown at him. *What? Someone has to ask.*

"I looked through her stuff and didn't find anything suspicious," Ivy responds. "I've probably already seen what the package held and didn't know it was what it was."

"Does she have any enemies?" I ask, and Ivy laughs through her tears.

"This is some real CSI hardcore questioning," she says. "But yes, I've thought about it. The police asked the same thing. The students who die in school? They die in fraternity initiations, in accidents. In crimes committed by strangers. Suicides. Meryl was not interested in sororities. And she wouldn't end up in the FA building because of an accident, would she? So it's either a crime. Or a suicide."

I take a deep breath. "The body was already decomposing when they—"

"So we can only guess at this point," Ivy says. "And I've seen those prints. She was not happy."

But she was not the girl in the building.

Before long, Ivy and Louis are clearing the table, talking about lighter things: gardening ("Everything I plant dies," Ivy says), cooking a chicken breast without drying it out, and the hidden charges in college tuition.

"Oh, speaking of which," Ivy says. "Why didn't you tell me you used to teach at the University?"

I look at her and at Louis, wondering if this oversight will lead to a suspicion of some sort. But Ivy looks at us with a pleasant smile.

"I told Leslie about falling off the bike and she asked for your names and where the house was," Ivy continues. "She said you used to teach Investments and Fundamental Accounting. She was actually classmates with Meryl and Arman in Accounting when they were sophomores." She looks at us, hoping for an anecdote or a look of recognition. I am trying my hardest to keep a poker face but I must have looked lost because she says, "You probably don't remember them."

"The classes were big," Louis says.

"But I suppose you remember Kayla?"

Our faces show a big fat *No*. "Oh," Ivy says, looking confused now. "I thought you'd remember her, Louis. She was SA for several semesters and she said you emailed her early this year asking if she knew a student who's interested in house sitting."

"Ah, Kayla," Louis says. "Of course." It is a lame attempt; I don't know if Ivy catches on.

"Yes, she said you were going on a long vacation with your brother and you were worried about your plants." She smiles wider, as though the detail amuses her. "Then later on you said it's okay because Jonah's already found someone."

I almost asked, *Who? Who did I hire?*

"For the record," Ivy says, "I can be an excellent house sitter." She and Louis share a laugh, and Louis says, "I'll keep that in mind."

Ivy leaves the house with the Pyrex bowl, already washed and dried by Louis. She holds it against her stomach as if it were a book. She says she'll be using her brother's car for the rest of the month, with her poor bike out of commission. Louis tells her it's probably for the best. "Bye," she says cheerfully when her cab arrives, and we raise our hands, wave a desultory wave.

"You hired a house sitter," Louis tells me, facing the departing Ivy with a rigid smile on his face, even before he can lower his hand.

I wake up in the middle of the night and the knee immobilizer is gone.

I flex both legs and swing them over the side of the bed. I accept this all, I accept this even as my lucid mind tries to tell me this makes no sense. I tell my body to wake up but my voice is pathetic. It hums too softly, like an animal beneath the floorboards, like a body in the basement.

The basement. I go down to the basement with a ratty bed sheet. Maroon, the color of old blood. I spread it on the floor of the basement like a picnic blanket.

I open the chest freezer and look at Meryl through the haze of freezer fog. I marvel at the sight of her, but only for a second. I lift her out and place her in the center of the maroon sheet. Her arms are folded over her chest. She is as light as a bird.

I bundle her up like dirty laundry. Like garbage. I bury her in the backyard. I feel the sweat on my back and arms and the strain in my legs and biceps as I dig a hole for her.

I feel relief.

I feel relief.

I wake up on my own bed, in the dark, and feel the relief leave me, like a blanket sliding off on a cold night. I turn my head and see a naked girl, her arms folded over her chest, standing in one corner of the room.

I wake up, for real this time. The sunlight looks stronger than usual. The clock says 10:30 am. Louis has let me oversleep.

He barges into the room. I push myself up against the pillows, blinking against the light.

"You didn't wake me up," I say.

He ignores me, and strides to the window to fix the curtain.

"Come on," he says, turning to me with the wheelchair. He glances at the curtain again, makes sure the windows are covered. "Someone's coming."

"Who?"

"Students," he says.

I wheel myself to the doorway of my bedroom, straining to hear them through the open front door. I hear a put-on disappointed groan. Soft laughter. Louis appears at the door, turns back to wave goodbye—*"Bye! Tell him to get better!"* someone calls out—and finally enters the house.

"They heard from Ivy that you were in a wheelchair," Louis says. "They heard about the accident but didn't know where you were staying. They said they went to your apartment building, but the guard said you weren't there. Otherwise, they said, they would have visited right away."

He is carrying a small plant in a white ceramic pot, the leaves white-edged and triangular. English Ivy. Ivy snaking her way into our lives by telling everyone everything. "They brought this for you," Louis says. He hands the plant to me and wheels me back into my room. I place the ivy on top of the study table.

Something he has said earlier shakes me awake. "Apartment building?"

"Yes. I actually asked them about it, pretended I didn't know." Louis tells me the name of the building, and the apartment number.

"I'm not familiar with the place," he says, "but I can look it up. Hopefully it's reachable by cab."

"Did they tell you their names?"

"They didn't have to," Louis says. "They're the kids from Ivy's video. Leslie, Kayla, and Arman. I told them you were sleeping. Maybe you're good with students, made an impression on them. They're genuinely worried about you."

I lift the pot and examine it. The ivy is in a mix of potting soil, sand, and peat moss, the top layer covered with smooth white pebbles. It looks like an expensive arrangement.

"Do you think they would know about our house sitter?" I say.

"I asked them about that, too." He lay back on the bed with a grunt. "They don't know. They looked at me funny. They probably think I hit my head too hard during the accident."

"So no one knows who we hired," I say. No one but us. "Do you think it's a student?"

Louis sits up. "I asked the guy who brings our groceries and our old cleaning lady. They don't know, either. They just started working for us when we got back from Cebu, apparently. Would you like me to put that near the window?"

He reaches for the plant and I hand it to him. Louis stands up and walks to the window. He pushes the curtain aside to let sunlight in, and places the ceramic pot on the low bookshelf. He stands there for a few more seconds, just looking at the plant.

"What's wrong?" I ask.

Louis rushes back to me, carrying the pot with both hands. "There's something here."

It must have glistened with the white pebbles, reflecting the sunlight. I pull it out. A small glass tube, about an inch long, has been pushed into the potting mix. A tiny part of the smooth end is visible through the loam, peeking through when it changed hands and the movement upset the soil. Inside the tube is a rolled-up piece of paper, which falls on my lap.

I roll it out and feel blood rush to my head when I read the words.

hope you got rid of the body

13

The message is typewritten. Premeditated, yes, but also desperate. Desperation leads to dangerous measures. Dangerous measures are reckless. What if someone else saw the glass tube? What if it was never discovered? Whoever sent the message didn't care; the message simply had to be sent.

I'm still operating on the assumption that a student is involved.

"They said the gift is from your students in Fundamental Accounting," Louis said. "Ivy said Arman, Leslie, and Meryl were in one class. We knew Kayla because she was a student assistant at the college. I don't know if she ever became our student."

"Did they say whose idea it was to bring me a plant?"

Louis shakes his head.

"It could be someone other than the three who dropped by," I say. "Or a faculty member." Or the proprietor of the shop where they bought the ivy. Or anyone else in the world, for that matter. I feel my fingertips go cold, the panic settling in. "Someone *knows*, Louis."

He exchanged numbers with Ivy the day she fell off her bike; he sends her a text, asking for the students' numbers. There are several numbers in Louis's phone, several names we don't recognize. Some of the numbers might belong to other students. I itch to send them all a message. *Who did we hire? Who else stayed in this house and knew about the chest freezer?*

We hear a tone. The numbers have arrived.

"What will you say?" I ask. Louis shows me what he has typed: *I haven't.* A cryptic enough message that will not get us in trouble if read out of context. Louis presses Send, and we wait, sitting in my room, staring at the ivy on the study table.

The replies come, almost immediately, almost at the same time.

Kayla: *Huh? Who's this?*

Arman: *Wrong send? Who's this?*

Leslie: *Who's this pls?*

Louis drops his phone on the table in frustration.

The phone beeps again about a minute later. Louis sits back up and checks his phone.

"What?" I say, my heart banging in my chest. "Is it a text?"

It is from a number not listed in Louis's phone directory. He tries to call it. When he lowers the phone again the voice coming from the receiver is loud enough for me to hear. *The number you have dialed is either unattended or—*

The message is short, angry: *you goddamn idiot*

"It's one of the three kids," I say. Louis brings toast, water, coffee, and his laptop into the room. I take a few bites of the toast he shoves at me and take my pain medication with a glass of water. Everything tastes like cardboard.

Louis looks at me without saying anything while the laptop boots up. I think he's waiting for an explanation. "One of them used another SIM card to reply," I continue.

"Or," he says, "it's not even a reply and it was sent by someone else."

"So the culprit just got up and decided randomly to text us that we're goddamn idiots," I say. "That sounds complicated. Occam's razor?"

"Occam's razor says *we* did it," Louis says. "We're in the damn house."

"I dreamt that I buried her," I say. Louis, absorbed in whatever he is reading onscreen, says, "Huh?" without looking up. I don't repeat myself.

I glance at the screen. He is loading several tabs. "What exactly are you looking for?"

"All of these kids are online now," he says. "Some of them don't even bother locking their accounts. They think that one little corner of the Internet is private enough."

Leslie and Arman's Facebook pages are largely empty, save for a few news links and human-interest pieces for Leslie, fiction and movie review links for Arman, and school-related kvetches for both. Kayla's account is more active, with posts about college activities and university announcements, travel photos ("Singapore 2012!!!"), family birthdays, and dinners with classmates.

Leslie, Arman, Meryl, and Mona are among the commenters on one of Kayla's posts about enlistment. Louis clicks on Meryl's name. Her page is filled with messages that have pushed down her own content. "I hope to god it's not you." "I hope you're okay, M." "Praying, praying, praying."

Louis scrolls down. Meryl's posts were mostly images of paintings and sketches with their source links. No mention of the hell she was living through inside her body. It appears that she poured her heart out into her planner instead of on the Internet.

Louis goes back to Kayla's page and clicks Mona's name. Mona has no profile picture. The link leads to the Facebook home page.

"She deactivated her account," Louis says.

Louis spends another hour or so scrolling down pages. I am close to nodding off on my chair when he nudges my shoulder.

"Look at this," he says. Onscreen is Meryl's page. He points at a message Kayla has posted on Meryl's Wall back in late November: STOP TALKING TO HER.

No one has commented on the message status. Either no one saw it, or no one wanted to join in the fray.

"What was that about?" I say.

"Probably nothing," says Louis, taking out his phone. "Probably everything."

"What are you doing?"

"What *you're* doing, you mean," he says. "You're calling Kayla."

Louis puts the call on speaker. While the phone rings, I say, "Why me?"

"You're the star professor," he says. "And you're the one they wanted to see this morning."

"But what will I say?"

"Just stay calm. Ask her about—"

But I will never be able to hear Louis's sage advice. Kayla picks up.

"Hello?" She sounds cautious, a bit annoyed. Kayla's environment is noisy.

"Kayla," I say. "It's Jonah?"

Like I'm unsure of myself. I clear my throat.

"Jonah!" she says, overjoyed. She moves away from the noisy crowd. "Hello, sir! Sorry about that, I'm in a seminar. But how are you! We dropped by this morning, but your brother said you were asleep."

I try to put some cheer in my voice. "Yes, he mentioned. Thank you very much for the ivy. It's in my room right now."

"Oh, was it ivy? I know next to nothing about plants." She laughs.

"Whose idea was it?" I ask. "To give me the plant?"

"Oh, wow I don't even remember. I just pitched in."

I don't know what to say next. Kayla fills the silence with, "I'm so sorry to hear about the accident. I hope you'll have a full recovery."

"Thank you," I say. "Um." Louis is jabbing a finger at the computer screen. "Listen, Kayla."

"Yes?"

"I heard about Meryl," I say.

"Oh, yes. It's terrible, isn't it?"

"And I have been looking at her Facebook page."

Silence on the other line.

"I just kept moving down the page, and I saw this message of yours."

"Okay."

"'Stop talking to her,'" I say, quoting her, and we hear a sharp intake of breath.

"Listen—" Kayla begins.

"What does it mean? Have you two been fighting?"

"It's about Mona."

In my mind flashes an image of a girl swan-diving from the top of a building.

"Back in November," Kayla says, "I saw Meryl talking to Mona. It was pouring and I was just leaving the Main Library when I saw them having a rather intense discussion outside."

"They were having a fight?"

"Not a fight." We hear her huff in frustration. "Meryl was asking Mona about Burnexa."

"What's that?"

"Diet pills."

Louis and I stare at each other.

"Everyone knows Mona takes them," she says, "because she tells everyone. Burnexa is from Brazil and, sure, it causes weight loss, but it contains a lot of ingredients, including both uppers and downers. It causes mood swings, personality changes. It's also carcinogenic and can damage the muscles of your heart. It's banned by the FDA. It's *bad*, sir."

"How come you know all this?" I've never even heard of Burnexa.

"I took it." There is defiance in Kayla's voice. *Yeah, so, what will you do about it?* "For a month or so. Back when I was a sophomore. I got it from a cousin who lives in South America. I lost more than twenty pounds and it made me paranoid. I couldn't even leave my bed without checking for listening devices inside my pillows."

"My God, Kayla."

"I know. So I tried to warn Meryl. I sent her an email but she told me to mind my own business. I posted on Facebook even though it's incredibly tacky because I was so desperate to get her attention. Even then, no reply. A friend saw it and thought it was a bug and asked me if my account had been hacked." She laughs without humor.

"Did you see them talking after the library? Does Ivy know?"

"I don't know if Ivy knows. If Ivy knew, she'd be the first to shake some sense into Meryl, believe me. And no, I didn't see them together again after that."

"Could the pills be the reason Mona jumped?"

Kayla pauses for a moment, thinking. "That's possible," she says. "My lowest point was cutting my pillows open with a box cutter but I was *this* close to slitting my own throat."

"I need a drink," I say.

It has started to rain. I can't remember the last time I have seen rain in this place. The noonday sun disappears behind thick clouds and the street looks the way it looks at 7 pm. Louis wheels me out on the porch and chugs down a glass of orange juice beside me.

"You don't drink," he says.

"It sounds like something you had to say in moments like this," I say.

We watch the rain for a while.

"The package," Louis says. "The package that Meryl got at the department. It was from Mona, wasn't it?"

I have deduced as much.

"I still don't understand how Meryl ended up here."

"We need to get rid of the body," I say, cringing when I realize I have just echoed the message in the rolled-up piece of paper.

"Yes," Louis says, suddenly, and I am surprised.

It doesn't matter what illegal thing we plan to do—we can't do much of anything anyway. The rain continues all throughout the afternoon. It is still raining when Louis begins setting the table for dinner. He turns on the TV and we listen to news about the southwest monsoon, about flooding in the city. We are used to rains, up north where we were born, but not to floods.

"Does it flood here?" I ask. I feel a tightening in my stomach when I imagine floodwater rushing down to the basement. To Meryl.

"I don't think so."

It is still raining after the dishes are put away. I almost admire the rain's tenacity, its unrelenting anger as it hits the rooftops. It produces a noise that can mask everything, even a speeding car, which we don't hear until Ivy's already parked out front and aggressively ringing the doorbell.

"What in the world?" Louis peers through the sheet of water pouring down the living room windows.

"What is she doing here?" From what I can make out, she is wearing a pink raincoat and black rain boots, and hugging a plastic-covered box to her chest. Louis meets her with an umbrella and puts an arm around her as they run to the front door.

She begins talking as soon as the door opens. "Her parents came to get her things and I found this under the mattress. I missed this the first time I looked through her stuff because I didn't think of looking there; I didn't think she'd keep anything there." She covers her face. "Oh my God."

"Slow down," I say, although I am starting to get scared. Louis has torn through the box's plastic covering while she is talking. Inside the box—a box that can indeed fit a note-book—is a disc, with a folded piece of paper. The paper is pink. Louis reads through it and hands it to me.

Meryl,

I can't stay here any longer. I don't know who else to trust. I'm sorry to leave you with this but you're the only person who actually spoke to me that one time I broke down in class.

I would have shown this to the police but I'm too scared.

You asked me why I was crying. Here it is.
Tell my mother I'm sorry.

Mona

"I began watching one of the clips but I can't finish it," Ivy says.

I find myself just staring at her. So, the package was indeed from Mona, but it didn't contain pills.

"You better get out of that raincoat," Louis tells Ivy, which shakes me out of my stupor.

"Let's hook up the DVD player," I say.

14

ouis prepares a huge mug of coffee for Ivy, but she doesn't want it. She sits on the couch facing the TV set and shivers under her jacket.

"I don't even know if I want to watch it," she says.

The DVD is a data disc. The clips are in numbered folders. Louis takes the remote and chooses folder #1. We see the single clip inside. The thumbnail shows a clear enough image to give us an idea of the video's subject matter but Louis presses Enter anyway.

The camera is focused on the girl's face. We can't see her body from the waist down. Her bright pink fingernails sink into the pillows under her head. Moans fill the living room.

Louis turns off the clip.

"That's Mona," Ivy says.

"This is the only clip you saw?" Louis asks. She nods. There are 37 folders in the disc.

"Do you think it's all Mona?" I ask.

"I don't know," Ivy says, beginning to tear up.

"It's okay," Louis says. "Relax."

He chooses a folder in the middle of the pack. The shot is off-center and shows only Mona's face, shoulder, and her bare breasts. "This is not fun anymore," she says. We wait to hear someone speak, but no one does. The camera keeps rolling for another minute. Mona is sobbing. "Stop pointing that fucking thing at me!"

Stop and Escape. Louis thinks for a minute. "Let's try the last folder."

Two girls on a bed. One wearing a man's shirt, the other naked save for a pair of pink panties. When the clip starts running, I am hit with a force of déjà vu so strong that I feel like vomiting.

They are kneeling on a bed facing a barred window. I know this. I have seen this before. The girl in the shirt slides her fingers under the garter of the other girl's pink panties. The girl in the shirt has her free arm around the naked girl's neck. The naked girl is trying to pull the other girl's arm down. The naked girl's fingernails are as pink as her underwear. Mona. Mona starts to cry. Who is the girl in the shirt?

Why did I dream about this?

"Damn it Mona," says the girl in the shirt, and Ivy puts a hand on her mouth. Ivy has recognized the voice. Who is it? We still can't see their faces. "You're no fun."

Mona is crying too hard to even get a word out. "I don't—I don't want—"

"But you enjoy this!" She throws an arm back and slaps Mona across the face. "You're the one who came to *me*. You wanted me to hit you as hard as I can, isn't that what you said that first time?"

Mona cries. "I want to go home."

"God*damn* it," the other girl says, frustrated.

We hear a man laughing. "Good Lord, you two," he says. His voice sounds familiar.

Mona turns to the voice, somewhere off-camera. "I didn't want to come here anymore, but she threatened to upload the videos. She'll ruin my life!"

"Jesus fucking Christ," says the girl in the shirt, who slides off the bed and disappears from the frame. "I am so done with you."

"I'm not," says the man, not laughing now, and I watch a pre-accident Jonah enter the frame, naked and erect, his legs whole and woundless, and pin a struggling and crying Mona to the bed.

There is no scream, no shocked interjection, just the three of us staring at the video. Seconds later, years later, I hear the rustle of Ivy's clothing as she stands up. "I think," she begins.

Denials go through my mind. *The person in the video is not me. I am not Jonah. I am not a monster.*

I am not going to hurt you.

"I think I have to go now," Ivy says.

I am on her left. Louis is sitting on the armchair on her right. Everything feels slowed down. "Ivy," I say, a warning both to her and to Louis, who is literally sitting on the edge of his seat, ready to move.

Ivy bolts, moving to her left, dodging Louis's hands. The mug lurches and falls to the floor on the carpet. The coffee spills. She hits my injured knee. I shout in surprise and pain, the edges of my vision turning gray. When the nausea passes, I see Louis and Ivy thumping across the living room floor and out onto the rain-soaked porch.

"*Help!*" Ivy screams into the storm as she runs on the driveway, but her voice is swallowed by the rain. I hear her still, a tiny sound: "*Help me! Help! Help!*"

I wheel myself to the door and notice someone standing beside the television.

A little girl in a white dress and a blue-and-gold falcon mask.

It's the girl from across the street. What is she doing—

I stare at her. She lifts a finger to her mouth. *Quiet now.*

I start to cry as I recognize her. How can I be so stupid? How can we be so stupid, letting anyone enter the perimeter?

"Louis!" I scream, my arms pumping as I turn the wheels. I reach the porch and feel the spray of rain on my face and body. "Louis! *Louis!*" Then I start screaming his real name.

This gets his attention. I see him turn around, an unconscious Ivy in his arms, and my wheelchair tips over. Is she doing this? Is she punishing me now? I put my arm out to brace my fall. I land hard on the porch, banging my knee again, my ruined knee, and black out for I don't know how long.

When I open my eyes, Louis is standing between me and—

"Auntie," he says. "Auntie, you need to let us explain."

Auntie. Leonora, but we have always known her as Auntie. Grandfather's cousin from the branch of the family tree that got slaughtered during the war. She is a survivor, and she is a constant. She is terrifying.

I see her in her true form in front of Louis, a full head taller than him, the skirt of her long black dress glistening with gems—the blue and gold of the little girl's falcon mask. There is no little girl. There has never been a little girl, just a spy from the estate.

"Please," Louis says. "He's already hurt."

Auntie doesn't say anything. After a moment, she raises her hand and Ivy floats up from Louis's arms and into the house. "Hurry up," she says, following the levitating girl.

Louis rights the wheelchair and helps me up. "Louis," I say. "We're—" *Dead,* is what I want to say, but I have to grit my teeth against the pain as Louis pulls me up and onto the seat. I can imagine my broken bones grinding loosely under my skin. I feel like throwing up right there on the porch, but I end up coughing instead. My face and arms are slick with sweat despite the cool air and the heavy rain.

"Are you all right?" Louis asks.

"Louis," I say again. My voice sounds like it's coming from a deep well.

"It's okay," he says. "We'll be okay."

Auntie is standing by the windows looking at the rain when we go in. Louis wheels me back to my earlier spot and sits on the armchair beside me. Ivy is on the couch, still unconscious. There is clotted blood on her hairline.

With her back still to us, Auntie raises her hand, and several things happen at once. The door closes, the curtains are drawn, the mug and the spilt coffee rise from the floor and return to the table, the couch carrying Ivy moves until it is behind us in a dark corner of the room, and the armchair across from us pulls itself back to make room for Auntie. She walks across the living room and sits down, folding herself into the chair, gracefully, like a dancer. Like water. And like water, her gaze flows from the top of my head to the tip of my toes. She turns her gaze to Louis, who does his best not to look away. I look away.

90

True beauty inspires awe and fear. It incapacitates. It knocks the air out of your lungs. And Auntie is beautiful.

"Lovely house," she says, sitting back, her hands resting on the arm rests, just a visitor enjoying the night's conversation. She looks at Louis. "Lovely perimeter. It gave me pause, I have to say. Forced me to make sure. I truly appreciate the effort. It was flimsy, though. And useless, in the end."

Louis takes a deep breath but doesn't say anything.

"My lovely boys," she says. "But I prefer your old faces. I suppose your discarded bodies are already buried?"

We don't answer. We don't know.

"What do you call yourselves now? Jonah? And Louis?"

Silence, ominous and heavy, hangs over us, until I can take it no longer and I nod my head. Louis turns to stare at me as though I have betrayed him.

Auntie places an elbow on the armrest and cups her chin. "The names of the brothers you have murdered."

The last word makes me jerk. "Auntie—"

"Tell me about body-snatching," she says, cutting me off.

"It is," I say, my heart hammering in my chest, "it is illegal."

"It is _immoral._" She is not shouting—she never shouts—but my ears are ringing. "You have killed two young men in order to take over their bodies and their lives, and what right do you have?"

Words from our childhood. "We have no right," I say.

She nods. "You have no right."

"But Auntie—" Louis begins.

"No exceptions," she says, and in my head I hear an annoying uncle saying, It is 'Thou shall not kill. Period', not 'Thou shall not kill, unless—'.

Unless you meet a charming young college instructor who sexually assaults his students.

"You need to hear why we did it," I find myself saying.

"I am not interested," she says. "It doesn't change what you have done."

"If we didn't do it, you'd kill us anyway."

"Then you should have just faced death."

I wipe my eyes. Is there no mercy, no mercy at all? "And Celeste?" I say.

"Celeste's dead," Auntie says, as though everything is that simple. Just black and white.

"I wish I could see the world your way," I say.

Auntie leans forward, crosses her legs, and folds her hands on her knee. I brace myself for a sharp rebuke, or better yet, a flick of her finger that will break my neck.

But instead she says, "The family wants you back."

What?

"What?" I say. "That's impossible. After everything that's happened, Father would never—"

"Your father is dead."

I fall silent. I feel Louis's hand on my shoulder. For a moment I feel nothing—my father and I have never been close—but I remember my mother, alone now in that big house, and I feel an ache in my chest, the sting of tears behind my eyes.

"It was his heart," Auntie says and I think, *Pain is bad for the heart.* That night, my father must have suffered an insurmountable amount of pain.

"With your father gone, you are now head of the estate."

I can't imagine facing the family, facing my mother, with my new face, my new name.

"Do they know," I say, "what we did after we left?"

Auntie stares at me for a few seconds and says, "No."

"Maybe you should tell them first."

"Your mother wants you back. I suppose a pardon is in order."

"And you'd allow that."

She stares and stares. "My opinion bears no weight in this matter," she says.

"Whatever happened to 'no exceptions'?" I say, brave now, but not brave enough to push it when she doesn't rise to the bait.

I ask, "What will happen to Louis?"

She still doesn't reply, but I can deduce enough from her silence.

"If we went back with you," I say, feeling an ugly need to spell it out, "Louis will be put to death."

Auntie looks at Louis, looks at me. Still, she says nothing.

"Either we will both be put to death, or we will both be allowed to live," I say. "Because if I was pardoned and Louis was not, how will that look to the rest of the estate?" *How can I be head of the estate if I have a face nobody can recognize?*

"You have to go back to tell Mother," I say, "and ask her how she wants to proceed."

"I am hoping you can go back with me so you can tell your mother yourself." She nods at the couch behind us. "But I see that you have loose ends to tie."

Ivy. Meryl. I wonder if Auntie knows about the basement, if she can read my mind, right now. As children we believed she could do that, which made her more terrifying in our eyes.

Right now, I can't say for sure.

She stands, and Louis stands with her. I would have done the same—I actually leaned forward, only to feel my legs tying me down like boulders—because old habits die hard.

"Tomorrow," she says. We nod. She looks at Louis. "Your father is grieving."

"I know," he says.

"I will need to tell him as well."

"Yes."

She moves as if to turn to the door. At the last moment she pauses, steps forward, and places a finger on my knee. She puts no pressure on it—it is so light her finger could have been hovering—but I nearly scream.

"I can mend your bones," Auntie says. Louis has taken a step forward with his hands slightly raised, as though planning to tackle her.

I nod, but in my head, I am screaming *take your finger off take it off take it off take it off*—

"I can," she says, "but I won't. Do you understand why?"

They were nearly the same words she told me when I fell from Grandfather's tree when I was eight. *Your mother has told you several times to stop climbing this tree. I can fix this, but I won't. Do you understand why?*

I do. I nod. *Because I don't deserve it.* She turns without another word and steps out the door, the imagined weight of her finger like a brand on my knee, the sound of the rain spiriting her away.

Louis sits down again. I can hear him cursing under his breath. I have no anger left; in a strange way, I am relieved. What was bound to happen has happened. Now I can move on, now I can stop hoping. Hope is a fragile thing, but it is a heavy thing, and the pain in my bones is heavy enough as it is.

Ivy begins to moan, first like a person awakened from a dream, then like a person injured. Louis stands up, goes into his room, and comes back out with a pen and a notepad. Ivy touches her forehead and sits up. Louis starts to draw something, but I touch his arm, shake my head. This is mine. I take the pad, draw the necessary symbol, and tear off the page. Ivy screams, tears flowing down her face (*Help help help me please help*), and abruptly falls silent when I hand her the piece of paper. She takes it and sighs, shoulders slumping, muscles and mind starting to relax.

"You raped Mona," Ivy says. No hysterics. No anger. No fear.

"No," I say. The calm is a welcome change. "I'm in Jonah's body, but I am not Jonah."

Louis sits beside Ivy with the first-aid kit and begins to clean her wound. She doesn't flinch.

"I loved Meryl, you know," Ivy says.

"I know."

"But I didn't tell her because I didn't think she was interested in me that way," she says. The tears fall again, but she no longer sobs. She looks at me. "I should have told her."

I take her hand. "I'm so sorry, Ivy."

She frowns, thinks. "You're not Jonah?"

I need her like this, slow and vague, but receptive. Or else she'll be clawing out my eyes, running screaming into the rain again.

"No," I reply.

"Are you sure about this?" Louis says. The lid of the first-aid kit clicks shut.

"I don't know," I say. But I do know. Either we tell her or we kill her.

I decide to tell her.

Let's say my name is Jonah and he is Louis.

*Even here, in this story, I can't make myself
tell you our real names.*

PART TWO

The Mansion with the
Isolated Garden

15

I was nine years old the first time I saw someone die.

It was a bright February morning, very early, very cool, the morning light just beginning to touch the trees. *Bring the children so they'll learn*, Father said, and so we went. The whole family—aunts and uncles chatting, yawning, shaking their heads, arms draped over my younger cousins—stood in a secluded garden just outside the estate cemetery. I could see our home, the main mansion, in the distance, luminescent like a pool of water. My grandfather had his hand on my shoulder. The day had a festive air.

Two servants dragged the sugarcane farmer in front of us. Auntie stepped forward and asked in a clear, crisp voice, "What is your name?"

The farmer said his name. Auntie glanced over her shoulder, and Grandfather looked at her and shook his head.

"When did you start working for us?" Grandfather asked him. The farmer replied, and Grandfather scoffed. "You're off by about eleven years."

"What is your daughter's name?" Auntie asked. The farmer couldn't reply.

"Why do you continue to lie, Manolo?" Grandfather said.

Manolo, my Father's youngest brother. One of my uncles. But I knew him as a tall young man with the sarcastic grin, the rebel at the dinner table who kept ruffling Grandfather's feathers. He was definitely not this old man with the sunburnt face.

Manolo's body was found in one of the sugarcane fields three days ago.

"You couldn't blend in," Auntie said. "The farmers gave you up."

"It was an accident," my uncle Manolo said through the old farmer's mouth. "Father."

"An accident where you find yourself in someone else's body?" Auntie said.

Manolo ignored her. "Father," he said. "Just let me go. Let me leave the estate. Let me live my remaining days as this old man. No one has to know."

"The old man knew, Manolo," Grandfather said. "His daughter knows. His *grandson* knows."

"It was an accident!" he said. "I swear to you."

Later, when we were old enough and brave enough to talk about it, Louis and I decided that Manolo planned to take a younger man's body but ended up with the old farmhand by mistake, so it really was "an accident."

He tried to run, that fine morning in the garden. Manolo bolted to the trees, nearly dragging the servants with him.

Auntie lifted a finger, and we heard a soft crick, like the sound of a gate swinging shut or a twig split in half, and Manolo fell on the grass.

"Return the body to the family," Grandfather said, and we walked back, dry-eyed, to the main mansion. Breakfast was waiting.

Gossip circulated among us cousins about our uncle, speculations on why he did what he did: he met a girl in the town proper, he wanted to move to Manila, he learned that he had a tumor in his brain and would be dead in a fortnight. We never found out. It didn't matter. What he did was *wrong,* and if we did the same thing, Auntie would break our necks and our family wouldn't even shed a tear.

Let's say my name is Jonah and he is Louis.

Even here, in this story, I can't make myself tell you our real names.

16

Ten years ago, the estate was bigger than this city. Bigger than this city twice over. Five families lived on the estate—my grandfather's sons and daughters, and their spouses and children. My grandmother had passed on when Celeste was still an infant. I have no memory of her. Leonora, Auntie, lived alone in a house near the farmers' housing complex. My father was the eldest, and our family lived with my grandfather in the main mansion. My uncle Manolo was unmarried, and so he also lived with us. When he died, my father turned his room into an adoration chapel.

Surrounding the main mansion were the vast sugarcane fields. A sugar mill. Our own little hospital, a marketplace, a church, housing for the farmers, even a school for their children. It was its own country. Grandfather ran it the way it was run by his father, and his father's father: like a welfare state, providing free food, education, and healthcare to everyone employed within its confines. But for many years, Grandfather ran the sugar mill at a loss. Fortunately, he had other investments, other businesses outside the estate, and the money coming from those ventures sustained the family's sugar business.

Most of the house servants, the farmers, the grounds superintendents, the gardeners, the drivers—my Grandfathers' longest-serving and most treasured employees—knew what our bloodline could do. But they kept this information to themselves either out of loyalty or fear.

Celeste, my sister, was the eldest. I was born two years after her, and my twin brothers, Paulo and Samuel, were born twelve years after me. I always thought of the twelve intervening years as my parents' period of rumination. *Should we have another child? Should we try again?* They answered yes and they had two in one go. Everyone in the family was delighted. They said the bloodline never had twins before and it could be a herald of good things to come.

Everything hurts in hindsight.

Louis is the only son of my father's brother—my grandfather's second son. We were all homeschooled, my siblings and cousins and I, with Auntie as our governess, helped by several hired tutors. It's not like we were cooped up in the estate like prisoners all our life. We went on trips, sometimes abroad, and homeschooling was the best way for us to remain on schedule.

We were also taught—

I don't know what to call it.

Tricks? We were also taught tricks, like the symbol on the piece of paper. Like Louis's perimeter fence. For our protection.

We were never taught the stronger spells. Like taking over bodies. Grandfather talked to his children about it, showed them our ancestors' notes, the terrible things that had happened because of it, hoping to dissuade them from even trying. And yet, look what happened to Manolo.

These handwritten journals were still in the library, hidden, restricted, closely guarded, in its bowels.

They should have just burned those journals after Manolo died, but my Grandfather was a champion of Family and History.

This was how I had always pictured my life: My education at home would end at the secondary level, though the tutors would start teaching me finance, people management, and the structure of the family business when I turned 15. I would take an extensive trip around the estate and, eventually, leave to see our offices in the province and in Manila when I turned 16. I would move to the city to work on my college degree. While taking classes, I would work for the company so I'd know more about the family business. I would get my diploma at age 21, return to the estate, marry one of my cousins, oversee whatever part of the business my father would entrust to me, live in one of the mansions, have children, and die.

It was the only life I know and the only life I learned to want.

The year I turned 16, the year I was supposed to leave the estate for college and the larger world, my grandfather died.

It was like a siege ring closing.

17

*G*randfather was a healthy man. I've seen him felled by a fever at least once or twice in my lifetime, but even in his late 60s he would still go jogging or biking around the estate with his dogs, saying hi to the farmers and making his children nervous. As he got older though, he started complaining about aches and pains in various body parts. His hip, his joints, his head, his eyes. He started walking with a cane.

The year I started learning about income tax, one of the servants found him on the floor of his bathroom, bleeding from a head wound. He said he had slipped. He disliked doctors and hospitals, and allowed only Auntie to tend to his wound and his aching hip. He insisted that he just needed to lie down to recover his strength. His self-imposed bed rest stretched to two days, then five, then eleven. He got angry whenever my father and his siblings talked about getting a doctor and eventually banned them from entering his room. His grandchildren were welcome, however, and my cousins and I visited to keep him company. Louis and Celeste, along with my other older cousins who were already in college, returned to the estate whenever they could.

I read books to Grandfather or we'd read to ourselves, quietly, him propped up on the bed and me on a chair. I was halfway through *Lord of the Flies* when he realized he was too weak to even sit up.

A lot of things went wrong, all at once. He was like a machine with failing gears. First his kidneys, then his liver. The doctors and nurses came then, along with the dialysis machine. The pain medication. Louis and I would sit in grandfather's bedroom, the twins on our laps. One night, Louis was explaining to the twins what he does at the office in Manila ("assisting with business development and risk management"—effectively putting the twins to sleep), when Celeste walked in. It was a Saturday but she had Saturday classes. We didn't expect her.

"What are you doing here?" Louis asked.

"How is he?" Celeste said, shedding her backpack.

I jumped when I heard Grandfather answer. "Alive," he said, though his voice betrayed his frailty. "Still alive, Celie. Come here."

Celeste sat on the bed and kissed his cheek. Grandfather's hand rested on Celeste's arm, fingers trembling like paper fluttering in the wind. "Good," she said. She looked back, saw that the twins were asleep, and said, "Look how sick you are, Lolo. Explain to me again why Auntie can't heal you."

"I am old, Celie," Grandfather said. He sounded jovial, but I saw him withdraw his hand from Celeste's arm. "This is what happens when you grow old."

"Not if Auntie can help it."

"Celie," Louis said. "Let Lolo have his rest."

"You can't interfere with Life's natural process," Grandfather said, serious now. "You know that, Celeste."

That was another thing he was a champion of. Life's Natural Process.

"You mean God. God's will."

"Yes, Celie."

"But it's okay to learn how to draw a symbol to put my noisy roommate to sleep," my sister said. "So are we or are we not supposed to interfere with Life's Natural Process with these spells or not? This family confuses me."

"We're teaching them for your protection," Grandfather said. "Not for you to abuse."

"So, there are loopholes."

I lost my temper then. I asked her what she was doing, but she ignored me.

"Pain is not natural," Celeste told Grandfather.

"Oh?" Grandfather said. At this point he was still humoring her.

Celeste said, "You know there's a way to escape this. Tito Manolo knew, but you were too stubborn to understand."

I went rigid. Louis stood up, Samuel sleeping in his arms. "Celeste," he said. "Stop it."

"Why are we even given this ability if we're forbidden to use it?" Celeste said. "What was the point?"

"You would kill a person," Grandfather said, "in order to continue living in a new body?"

107

"I go to the sugar mill," Celeste said, "get involved in a terrible accident, break both of my legs. Nearby is a farmer with no family. An orphan. No roots in the world. Wants to die anyway. You wouldn't let me take over his body? You'd let me suffer and die with broken legs because of Life's Natural Process?"

Grandfather was getting angry, his face going red, eyes bulging. But instead of shouting at Celeste to get out, he started to cough, a dry, hacking cough that sounded like thunder. Louis grabbed Celeste's arm and dragged her away, calling for the nurses. I followed them out of the room. Paulo woke up in my arms and asked why we were fighting.

18

e still don't know how our uncle Manolo got his hands on the journal of forbidden spells, but we know Celeste found it inside the mansion when she helped Father clear Manolo's bedroom of his belongings.

She showed us when Louis confronted her after her outburst in Grandfather's bedroom. We had already tucked in the twins and we were standing just outside their door, in the dark hallway. The mansion was silent, save for Grandfather's dogs barking at each other downstairs. People had gone either to bed or to pray in the chapel, like my parents.

Celeste opened her backpack and took out a small leatherbound book that looked like it had been unearthed from a grave.

We looked. Of course, we looked. We were scared but we were curious. Story of all of our lives, right?

We looked at one page that night, the one with diagrams and nearly incomprehensible words, and slept fitfully, waiting for Auntie to drag us out into the garden. When she didn't, when we woke up in our beds still alive, we read the rest of the journal, paying special attention to the instructions. *Best done in a supine position,* it said. *Relax,* it said. *Think of the blue sky.*

Three of Grandfather's dogs died. He got better. But you know what they say, right? That dying people get a little better before the end? Before long, we could hear him calling the names of his parents. They died during the Japanese attack on the estate in the Second World War but during those last few nights they were in the room with him.

Celeste wanted to help Grandfather, but the rule said the person leaving his body should be willing. And Grandfather wasn't willing.

Work in the sugar mill screeched to a halt when Grandfather died. We held the wake in the main mansion, the coffin at the foot of the grand staircase surrounded by light and flowers. All the workers in the estate waited in line for hours to view his body and pay their respects. I never saw Auntie cry, though at the burial she stood for a long time by the coffin, as though committing Grandfather's face to her memory before they shut the lid and lowered him to the ground. He was buried next to his parents in the middle of the estate cemetery. We buried him on a dry, windy day, the dust mingling with our tears.

Father took over, reluctantly. He was the eldest but he wasn't a very efficient businessman or a very good leader. He didn't muster the same respect Grandfather received effortlessly. His soft voice and restless eyes didn't easily command respect. Louis's father, who was given free rein to oversee business operations in the city even while Grandfather was still alive, would have been the better successor, but he was not the eldest.

Grandfather was the glue that held everything together, or else the shield that kept corporate machinations at bay. We controlled banks, a bus line, and a telecommunications company, the lifelines that kept the estate alive and allowed Grandfather to give our workers what they needed to lead a comfortable life. Just three months after Grandfather died and my father started attending board meetings, the takeovers began. Some politicians were involved, scumbags my Grandfather slighted by refusing to fund their reelections or some other damned thing. You know how this works. Investors lose trust, the family loses credibility, stock prices take a dive, and the monsters waiting in the wings take center stage.

Father claimed that he received death threats aimed at the family. *His* family, to be precise. So Celeste was called home and I never got the chance to step into a college classroom.

I was 16. Celeste was 18. The twins were four years old, and—blessedly innocent, blessedly clueless—were happy that their sister was home for an extended vacation.

The "extended vacation" lasted three years.

We lost the banks and the telecom company within a year. While the family fought for control of the bus line, the estate hospital ran out of medicine, and tools and machinery that broke in the sugar mill took forever to be replaced, if they were ever replaced at all. Father started downsizing. The teachers were the first to go, and with them went the promise of free education for the workers and their children. Uncle Pedro, Grandfather's third son and overseer of the sugar mill and sugarcane plantations, imposed longer hours on the farmers to increase production. Before long, my father was sending Celeste with Pedro to talk at the estate's monthly meetings. It took me a while to realize why: the farmers were getting angry and Father thought sending a young face, a face that symbolized a fairer future, would appease them.

Celeste always looked like a walking corpse whenever she came back from these meetings, her face pale, her eyes frightened. She refused to tell me why.

It was around this time when Father removed the televisions from the mansion, cut our Internet connection, edited the bookshelves in the mansion library, and threw out the "forbidden" books, including *Lord of the Flies,* the book I was reading when Grandfather was still alive. He said I was filling my head with garbage and God was punishing me through the family's businesses. My parents were Roman Catholic and we were raised Roman Catholic, but Father turned to his faith with such fervor that it became frightening. Celeste and I had frequent shouting matches with him until Mother fell ill, so we stopped fighting. Even the twins, sensing that my father could explode at any moment, stopped complaining about the cartoons they couldn't watch anymore, and prayed the rosary on their knees.

With the corporate takeovers, and my Grandfather's death, Father turned to a world he could control—his own house, where he still sat at the head of the table and where the checkbook still needed his signature.

Of course, this insight came to me in retrospect. At the time, I walked around with what felt like a boulder on my shoulder blades, thinking our lives were falling around our ears, and my father was going insane.

But then: Perhaps I was right about that, too. Especially considering what happened after.

19

ouis, who visited us often, offered to help us leave the estate. We could stay with him in the city until things settled down. But we couldn't leave Mother, and Louis's father, who was still somehow loyal to my father, would never allow it.

So we stayed, and the years marched on. We lost the bus line, we got buried in debt. The farmers went on strike, went back to work, went on strike again. Auntie joined Uncle Pedro in the talks after Celeste refused to attend the meetings. A lot of the workers left the property in the middle of the night, abandoning the farmers' housing complex. Creditors started calling and sending letters, wanting a piece of the dying property while my father and his siblings tried their best to ward them off.

I asked my sister why she refused to talk to the workers. I volunteered to go. She said she was just tired, and I should focus instead on taking care of Mother and the twins.

"Would you do it?" she asked, suddenly.

I was confused. "Take care of Mother and the boys?" I said. I thought I was doing that already.

"No. Leave me for dead with broken legs even if there's a chance I can take over another body."

It took me a moment to recall her conversation with Grandfather. Which, I must note, happened more than a year ago at this point.

"I don't know," I said. It was true. I really didn't know.

But she was no longer paying attention to me. She was looking away, lost in her thoughts.

"I hate my body," I heard her say.

"Don't say that."

"Do you think I'm pretty?" she asked.

"You are beautiful," I said.

"That's good."

She sounded like a person in a waking dream.

"Are you all right?" I asked.

"I feel dirty," she said.

I was just about to say something when she turned to me and asked, "Among our cousins, which one would you choose?"

I was very, very confused at this point.

"Which one?" she insisted. "Which body?"

I couldn't reply. I felt cold all over.

"I'm thinking Jessica." She was Uncle Pedro's only daughter. "She's younger, but she's slight, like me. Same height. It wouldn't be too disorienting."

"What the hell are you saying?"

Celeste frowned. "What?" she said, then shrugged and turned away from me. "Jessica," she said. "That's the one."

Louis was home for the summer the year I turned 19. He awakened me in the middle of the night and told me that Celeste was not in her room.

We looked for her in the twins' room, the kitchen, the dining area, the adoration chapel. She wasn't in the mansion. We didn't want to alert anyone else, especially Father, so we decided to head out to look for her ourselves.

I thought she had left the estate, and felt both mournful and glad. She deserved to be out of this constricting place, I thought.

If only.

We didn't have to go too far. Louis insisted that he heard a sound coming from the estate cemetery. We walked around the headstones for what felt like hours until I saw a glint of metal in the moonlight. Celeste was in the farthest corner of the cemetery, surrounded by trees, near the wall that separated the estate from the rest of the town. In this corner were the oldest headstones, weathered down by the centuries.

We found Celeste surrounded by our long-dead ancestors, digging up a hole. Digging up a grave.

We were so shocked we couldn't say a word. She was knee-deep in the hole, wearing a silk nightgown stained with grass and soil. She stopped to arch her back. That was when she noticed us. And that was when I noticed the girl lying on the grass beside the grave.

"Don't you dare," she said, picking up something from the ground and pointing it at us in one fluid stroke. She stepped out of the hole, using the shovel to boost her up.

"Where did you get that gun, Celie?" Louis said, and we saw our cousin Jessica lying there on the grass. This stopped us in our tracks.

"Same place I got the shovel and the sleeping pills," Celeste said. Her gaze hardened. "I'm doing this," she said. "All right?"

That was when our last conversation made complete sense. "You can't do this to Jessica," I said, finally finding my voice.

She responded by turning the gun on herself.

"If any of you interrupt me," she said, "I will shoot myself. Clear?"

She didn't wait for our answer. With the gun still trained on her right temple, she started reciting the words, words that we only saw in that handwritten journal that smelled of death. *This can't be happening,* I kept thinking. *This cannot be happening.*

I wondered then how desperate Uncle Manolo felt. How desperate and helpless and alone.

Jessica started to moan. We didn't know how long Celeste had been digging in the cemetery, but clearly the sleeping pills were wearing off. "What," she said, eyes fluttering open. "My head," she said, pulling herself up. "Celie? Celie, what did you do to me?"

Celeste did not miss a beat. She grabbed Jessica and placed a hand over her mouth before Jessica could scream. The gun was now pointed at us. We raised our hands. My sister continued with the incantation.

I would never forget Jessica's frightened eyes.

Louis leapt and tackled Celeste. All three of them fell into the hole. Lightning crackled in the distance. In its split-second light I stepped closer and called out: "Louis? Celie? Jessica?"

The first sound I heard was Louis crying.

Jessica was on her knees, with her back toward me, tangled up in Celeste's limbs. She touched her face, her hair. She started to laugh. "It worked!" It was Jessica's voice, but in it I heard my sister's deranged sense of wonder.

Celeste, clad in Jessica's skin, climbed out of the grave. Louis wouldn't get up. He sat there, catatonic, beside Celeste's body.

"Get up or I'll shoot," she said, pointing the gun at me.

"You are doomed, Celie," Louis said. He clambered out, moving like an old man. He shoveled dirt into the hole.

20

ouis and I fell asleep on the floor in the twins' bedroom, probably just out of sheer weariness, because I remember looking over at Louis at three in the morning and seeing him still staring wide-eyed at the ceiling.

I was frightened out of my wits but I couldn't process the grief and terror anymore. I had just helped bury my sister's body. I had just helped my sister slip into another home, which was her home now. It was too much. It was much too much. And so I fell asleep, and, eventually, Louis did, too.

The light was still weak when I felt someone shaking me. The twins, asking me what we were doing in their room, and why we were covered in dirt. That jolted me awake, and I nearly kicked Louis to wake him. We had to clean ourselves before the maids saw us.

Before my parents could realize that Celeste was missing, they became preoccupied with another tragedy. Uncle

Pedro was found dead in his room. There was an open bottle of sleeping pills on the bedside table, its contents scattered around it and on the floor. Everyone thought, *He overdosed. He made a mistake. He was suicidal.*

But there was blood and vomit on his chin and pillows. And then we found the note:

The first time he did it was after our meeting with the farmers. He threw me to the ground behind the sugar mill and said that was how he liked it, on the grass, under the stars. A true romantic, our Uncle Pedro.

He did it five more times after that, in this very same bed, while his children slept, until I finally mustered the courage to tell Father.

Who did not believe me.

Who thought I was making up stories so I would be allowed to leave the estate.

Who said I should be kinder to the "poor widower".

So I mixed cyanide with the poor widower's tea and smothered him with a pillow.

Shame on you, Father. Shame on you, Pedro, devil, viper. Shame on this family.

C.

I ran out of the room and threw up in the corridor.

I don't remember much from Uncle Pedro's funeral. The family kept the police out of it. Of course, they did. The news mentioned "death from a brief illness".

One of my uncles said the cyanide crystals, which they used for fumigation until the mid-80's and now very occasionally as rat poison, was kept in a locked vault in Uncle Pedro's office in the sugar mill. They checked the vault and the crystals were gone. No one knew how Celeste got access, but everyone assumed she managed to leave the estate after murdering Pedro. No one noticed the patch of freshly turned earth in a corner of the cemetery, where my sister's body lay rotting.

My mother and the twins were inconsolable. Only the family accompanied Uncle Pedro during the wake. Nearly everyone left just after the first night, when we heard Jessica tell Father: "He did it to me, too. For years."

After that revelation, the maids could have rolled Uncle Pedro into an old *banig* and thrown him over the wall for all my Father cared.

"Can you believe that," Jessica (Celeste—let's call her Celeste) told me during the wake, "your Father only believed what your sister wrote after I spoke to him. So, he'd believe someone else's daughter before he could believe his own?"

Why didn't you tell me, I told her. Why didn't you tell me? It was all I could say. I started crying and she looked away, disgusted.

My memories of those final weeks in the estate were hazy. I remember only: the sticky sweet feel of the summer, Jessica seen in the distance like a mirage, the dust motes in the sunlight inside the library, the occasional rain, and the twins pulling me out to play under the downpour. Father was always out in meetings and Mother was always in her room, so I only had my little brothers as constant company inside the mansion. I still remember them jumping up and down in the rain, clambering on top of me to wrestle me to the ground.

They were so happy.

21

have not seen Jessica up close ever since Uncle Pedro's funeral, so when I saw Jessica in the vestibule on my last afternoon inside the estate, I moved away from her and nearly tripped on my feet.

Of course, I didn't know then it was going to be my last afternoon in my own home, but the dread was there, the feeling of something ending. There was another workers' strike. Louis and his father were with Auntie and my parents, trying to get a conversation going with the workers' leaders, trying to keep the media out of it. I was ashamed, frightened, and angry at how my father continued to cling to this notion that the estate operated as it did in the past, when Grandfather was still alive, when the workers still received the treatment they deserved, when people still treated each other like family.

"What's wrong?" Celeste said through Jessica's mouth. She was wearing a black dress and carrying a wicker basket filled with tin cans and a bag of chocolate chips. "One of the maids let me in but she disappeared back into the laundry room."

"Sandra," I said. "She's new." Most of the helpers had left or had been let go at that point. Dust had settled all over the mansion and there were weeds in the back garden.

Celeste herself looked like she had not been taking care of her own house. Jessica's skin and hair looked dull, and there were dark circles under her eyes. "I have not slept for nine days," Celeste said.

Up to this day, I still don't know whether she had been joking then or not.

"What's with the basket?"

She smiled, and for a split-second I saw my sister's eyes in Jessica's face. "I thought I might bake a cake with the twins," she said. Her smile dissolved and she looked suddenly tired, suddenly old. She wouldn't meet my gaze. "I miss them, you know."

I left her to set up in the kitchen, empty now of the family cook and her assistants, and fetched the twins. "Cake! Cake! Cake!" Paulo and Samuel chanted through the corridors. We found Celeste sitting by the kitchen table, her hand on her knees, looking pale and sick in the yellow glow. She was humming a song. The ingredients were arranged on the table, perfectly, as though they were going to be photographed: flour, milk, eggs, butter, sugar.

"Help me?" she asked when the twins approached her, and of course they wanted to help. Celeste took a handful of flour and blew a white cloud at their faces. The twins laughed. They pushed me out, playfully, tickling me as I walked backwards, and closed the door.

"We'll call you when it's done, *Kuya!*" they said.

I went to my room, planning to read a chapter or two from a book, but I ended up falling asleep. It was already dark when I woke up.

Cyanide kills by preventing the cells of the body from using oxygen. Because of this, its effect is greater on organs which use the most oxygen: the heart, the brain, and the lungs. Exposure to a large amount of cyanide, by any route, can lead to respiratory failure and cardiac arrest within minutes. Victims scream in excruciating pain before dying.

The twins' bedroom was empty so I headed straight to the dining room, imagining them eating their slice of chocolate cake and drinking their milk, imagining their reaction when I say, faux-heartbroken, *Why didn't you wake me up?* I imagined this as I walked down the stairs, despite the silence, despite the overwhelming silence that should have told me that something was wrong.

The dining room was empty. They must still be in the kitchen, I thought, they must have decided to eat at the kitchen table right after the cake popped out of the oven. And that was where I found them, Paulo and Samuel, curled on the floor, their chairs overturned.

I have visited this scene so many times in my head— the chocolate cake sitting like a bomb on its glass plate, the half-eaten slices on the table, the flour dusting the counters like ash fall—and I kept going back to those overturned chairs. They felt it immediately. The twins, my little brothers.

They felt it all at once. They screamed in pain, they suffocated. They placed their hands on their chests and their necks and tried to stand, but they fell to the floor, overturning their chairs. They felt it and they were gone before they could even understand what was happening. That was how they died: scared, confused, and in immense pain.

I should never have left them with her. I still have these terrible dreams, where instead of allowing the twins to push me out of the kitchen, I push back and wrestle the cyanide out of her hands. Then I wake up and I realize—

If only I had pushed back. If only I had stayed.

I would never forgive myself, for as long as I live.

You'd think a person like that would want to die himself. And yet here I am. Here I am.

I need to finish this story, Louis.

22

remember not full scenes but fragments:

The twins' bodies—they still feel soft and warm, so *alive*—pressed against my chest on the floor.

The maids arriving at the kitchen, hands over their mouths.

My knee hit the floor in the hallway as I fell in my haste and grief. I stayed there for a minute, as the panic escalated in the kitchen, until I remembered what I was supposed to do. I stood up and ran out of the mansion and across the field, screaming Celeste's name at the top of my lungs.

Whoever heard me probably thought that I had lost my mind. At the back of my head, a small voice whispered that Celeste was gone, I should be shouting Jessica's name instead.

I remembered the burial place my sister made for herself. That was how I ended up crossing the garden and entering the cemetery. Someone was howling. I followed the sound, and found Jessica in her black dress, her clothes stained with soil and flour and weeds, kneeling beside the grave. The grave had been dug open, and Celeste's body—face and limbs mangled by maggots and decomposition—lay visible in the hole.

The sight of my sister's body, green and black like rotting fruit, deflated my rage. I fell on my knees and burst into tears.

"This is what happens in the end," Jessica—Celeste—said, turning to me. "All bodies end up like this. The victim and the wicked decay the same way. Like they don't differ at all."

Her face, tear-streaked, shone pink in the moonlight. "There has got to be something better after this life, don't you think? Where we get our due? Otherwise," a sob gave her pause, "what's the point?"

"You poisoned the twins," I said, and a grief so great fell on my head that I felt rooted to the spot, even as I saw her move her hands, revealing Uncle Pedro's gun that had been there all along.

"I was going to shoot them," she said, "but I can't shoot them at the same time. That would mean turning to Paulo or Sam first while his brother watched. It was cruel. I couldn't do it."

"So, lacing a cake with poison makes it less cruel?" I said, the rage returning, growing.

"The twins love cake." She smiled through her tears.

"You have lost your mind."

"There is something better," she said, "after this life."

I lunged at her and placed my hands on her neck. She pulled the trigger in surprise, but the gun was aimed at the steel-colored sky, sending the bullet to the atmosphere. My ears rang. Her grip on the gun loosened as my hands around her neck tightened. The gun fell to the ground now, liberated, but I focused on her neck. My own enraged scream sounded strange and foreign to my ears. I watched her claw at my hands, watched her face change color, watched her eyes bulge. She believed in something better after this life but still fought the hands suffocating her. The body wants what it wants.

It was Jessica's body, Jessica's throat, Jessica's hands trying to pry my fingers loose, and right now Jessica was a stranger who broke into our home and killed my defenseless brothers.

Someone was calling my name, but it was background noise, a whistle under the roaring current of my anger. I ignored it until I felt arms slip under my armpits and try to pull me away.

It was Louis. He had to pull several times before he was able to yank me off of her. We staggered backwards and landed on our sides, on the ground, the impact sending a tremor up my elbow, the soil coating my arm and cheek. Later, I would find out that Louis was sent back to the main mansion because the talks fell apart and the workers were getting restless. He ran out when he thought he heard the sound of a gunshot.

I could hear Celeste cough; I could hear Louis saying something, over and over: The twins are dead.

Celeste, still coughing, was crawling toward the gun. I saw it sparkling like a puddle of water in the grass.

I sat up as if electrocuted. I was about to dive for the weapon when an explosion rang in the distance. Celeste and Louis turned their heads.

An LPG tank exploded in one of the houses in the farmers' housing complex. My father's guards, in their panic, thought it was the opening volley of an assault. They opened fire. Five were killed and twenty-three were injured in the ensuing stampede. I learned about this after the fact. The family was not able to completely keep the media out of it this time so there was coverage. I saw articles about it on the front page, but they were quickly pushed to the inside pages before disappearing completely.

That night, I didn't look back. The explosion gave Celeste pause, and gave me a split-second, a chance, to reach the gun first.

In the next moment I had the gun pointed at her. *There is something better after this life.* My sister believed that, in her heart of hearts, in her infinite sadness. I lifted the gun but did not pull the trigger. I don't know if I did it because I wanted to punish her, or because I still loved her.

But she reached for the shovel on the ground beside her and stood up to swing it, aiming for my head. I had no time to think. The gun was still in my hand, the barrel pointed at her head. I turned my eyes away.

I heard a wet, gurgling sound coming from Jessica's body. I had hit not her forehead or her face, but her neck. Celeste was choking on her own blood. I couldn't tell you how long I stood there, frozen in place. Louis came over, took the weapon from me, and stood over her. Before long, the gurgling sound stopped, leaving us with the aftersound of gunfire.

23

Louis dropped the gun as though it burned him. He turned to me, and later he said the expression on my face reminded him of how my mother sometimes looked at the dinner table. Like I had no more fight left in me. Like I no longer cared what happened next.

Louis said, "We need to get out of here," and that snapped me out of it. All we wanted was to get away from the bodies. As we drove away in his SUV followed by the noise of the stampede, and with the flames of the burning houses visible in the rearview mirror, we wondered if it would be better to burn all of our bridges.

At first, we thought we could make up a story. Wanting to avenge her father, Jessica killed and buried Celeste and poisoned the twins. She was poised to kill me as well, if not for Louis's help.

But would our family side with us? Would Auntie? Would Father, who found God and believed that murder is murder is murder?

If we were forgiven, would we be strong enough to deal with the fallout? After what was revealed after Uncle Pedro's death, Louis had spent more time outside the estate, as though trying to distance himself from what happened. I didn't have the choice or the luxury. Now, the twins and Celeste were dead. I couldn't imagine surviving a day in that near-empty house with an inconsolable mother and a father who would very likely respond to his grief by killing himself or killing his one remaining child.

I felt considerable relief as we drove away from the estate and the miles dropped behind us.

We drove for hours. We stopped thrice: once to strip the SUV of its plate number, once to eat, change our clothes, and sleep, and once to argue. About what to do. About where to go next.

But we both knew what the next step was going to be.

We started drinking. It was stupid but we needed something to dull our fears. It had been ten hours since I shot my sister. The road was nearly deserted until a sedan shot out of a side street and appeared in front of us. I remember laughing. I remember saying, Step on the gas and catch up to them before we lose our nerve.

We did not have time to see that the road feeds into a cul-de-sac.

I could start again, I thought, as we tailed the car. It was an amazing feeling.

PART THREE

Nothingplace

24

"And," I say, "here we are."

The rain continues. I feel extremely warm inside my shirt, but my hands are cold. While I am telling the story, Louis zips from one room to another, paces in the living room, looks out the window. He doesn't want to listen.

Louis stands beside me now. I hear the jingle of keys. He has the keys to Jonah's apartment in one hand.

Ivy is coming to, in a fashion. She still looks shell-shocked but her eyes, alive and aware, can now focus on mine.

"I'm so sorry," she says.

"You didn't know."

"Your poor brothers."

Louis turns away, walks to the window, walks back. Twice. Thrice. I wish I could do the same.

I have not told her everything. I have not told her about Meryl. I don't know if I want to, if I have to.

Louis leans forward and hands Ivy the incriminating disc back in its box. Ivy takes it calmly enough, but her lower lip trembles and her eyes glisten.

"Jonah is dead now," she says. She places the box on her lap and rests a hand on top of it. "The real Jonah. So I suppose justice has been served. But what about—What do we do *now?*"

Justice has been served. Maybe it's better if Ivy didn't know about the basement.

"I'm afraid we have to disappear for a little while," Louis says.

"I want to know what really happened," she says. *"She can't get away with this. I want to kill her."*

We don't hear the doorknob when it turns, but I feel a draft on the back of my head and suddenly the front door is open and there is someone standing there.

"You didn't ask for your key back after I finished house-sitting," says our visitor, locking the door behind her, "so I kept it."

The girl in the shirt, Jonah's partner.

Leslie.

25

She still has not seen the tableau in the living room. She turns, shrugs off her raincoat, and drops it on the floor with her bag. She bends to pull off her rain boots and that's when she sees us staring at her. She hesitates. Her eyes flit from Louis to Ivy, then to me. She smiles. She decides not to take off her boots. She tracks muddy boot prints into the living room, slinging her bag again over her shoulder.

"Ivy!" she says. "I didn't know you were here." She sees the DVD player hooked up to the TV set and the box on Ivy's lap, and her smile hardens like frost.

Ivy lunges at her, growling like an animal. Louis shouts in surprise. I hear slapping, high-pitched shrieks, then a stunned silence as Ivy and Leslie stand up. Leslie, face red from exertion, lips bleeding from a cut, is holding a gun.

Ivy sees this and begins to cry, the fight gone out of her.

Leslie blows hair away from her face. "I knew Louis would be here, but you? What the hell are you doing here, Ivy?" She chuckles. She pulls up her bag by the straps and takes out a roll of duct tape. "Take this and tape Louis to that chair over there."

"I don't have scissors."

"You're too cute," Leslie says, revealing a pair of scissors, snipping twice, taunting her. "You think I'll hand this to you? Get a move on."

I can try to ram her, but the damn coffee table is in the way. *Early weight-bearing is encouraged.* I grit my teeth, dig my elbows into the armrests, and try to pull myself up, one painful fraction of an inch after another.

"Try that and Louis will get it in the chest," Leslie says.

I sit back down, breathing hard. Leslie gives me a look before making Ivy sit on the couch. With one hand—her other hand holding the gun trained on Ivy's face—she duct-tapes her wrists and ankles.

"Interesting," she says, as Ivy whimpers. "When did you start caring about your brother?"

This gives me pause, and that's when I realize that Leslie and Jonah are partners-in-crime. She trusts him. At least, she did, once upon a time. And I have a character to play.

"It hurts too much to stand," I say, cautioning myself not to overdo it.

Leslie sits cross-legged on the coffee table. "You look like hell."

I look at her hair, her smeared eyeshadow. "Well, you don't look too hot yourself."

"That's not what you told me the last time I came here looking like this." She laughs, and my stomach churns.

"So," she says, "Louis. Nice to see you again. I was surprised when I heard that you actually brought your brother here. Ivy, do you know why Louis kicked him out? Jonah killed his *dog.*"

"Will you shut the fuck up?" I say. Is that what Jonah would say? I hope so.

"Buried him in the damn garden," Leslie continues. "You like that Louis? Flowers growing from the corpse of your beloved dog? Jonah here had a kick out of that. I'm surprised you didn't throw him down the basement stairs."

Leslie turns to me, winks. "What did you tell these two? That you are innocent? How the hell did they buy that?"

"I told them enough to keep them quiet for a day or two," I say. "Then you barge in here with a gun."

Leslie scoffs. "You're telling me they haven't seen the video yet?" She takes the box containing the disc from the floor. "Bet you just charmed Ivy here. Which is something, even for you Jonah, considering she doesn't even like dick."

Ivy cries. Louis strains against the duct tape.

"No one's screaming," Leslie says. "Despite your un-duct-taped mouths. I am impressed. But then who can hear you in this rain, right?"

"What are you doing here, Leslie?" I say.

"Tying loose ends," she says. "I thought today's as good a time as any to bury a body."

Ivy cries harder, but I don't think she completely understands. I stay quiet.

Leslie glances at Ivy. "Oh!" She laughs, amused. "You don't know, do you?"

Ivy looks confused.

"Ivy," Leslie says, "Meryl is in a chest freezer in the basement."

26

vy is dumbfounded. Leslie looks at her the way a mother would at a child that entertains her. *You dropped your toy again? You are so adorable.*

"No," Ivy says and Leslie begins to laugh. "You're lying."

But she need only look at us. Louis is grief-stricken but he can't react quickly enough to wipe the look of guilt from his face.

"What?" Ivy says. "I don't understand."

To my horror, Leslie takes out a tablet computer, slides her finger on the screen a few times, and turns the screen toward us.

I see Meryl's body for the first time. It is not the decomposing body that haunts my dreams. It is a photo of a person who has just died, eyes half-open, lips cracked and bleeding from dehydration and starvation.

Do not cry, I think. Do not look away.

"See?" Leslie says, as Ivy looks on with mounting revulsion. "Meryl finally got the perfect figure she wanted."

"This is a joke," Ivy says.

Leslie shrugs. "All right, then. It's not so much perfect as—"

"This is a joke! There was a body in the FA building! They found her bag and her necklace!"

"That was just some homeless girl I always saw roaming around campus," Leslie says. She tucks away the tablet computer. "I needed to stop the police from poking around, so I had this idea. The body size was correct. I offered her a beer. She was grateful and surprised someone even noticed her. It was sweet, really. She told me her name, but I forgot." She shrugs. "Jonah lent me a gun to shoot Meryl but I ended up not needing it. I didn't want to shoot this girl, though. Too messy, and there's the issue of the bullet lodging in her brain. So I laced her beer with Valium. Police didn't even look twice, did they? Typical. Just what I needed. They saw the jewelry and the bag and thought, Open-and-shut case. Time to go home."

"No," Ivy says as Leslie speaks, punctuating every sentence. "No."

"Yes," Leslie says. "You want to go to the basement, take a peek?"

"Shut up," Louis says, and Ivy's face crumbles.

"You took a photo?" I say, because I must remain in character. "How stupid can you be?"

Leslie huffs. "Not so stupid as to keep a body as long as you did."

I hear Ivy's breath hitch. "All those times I came here—All those times I—" She cannot finish her sentence.

Leslie shakes her head in sorrow. "Monsters, aren't they?"

"What did you do to her?"

Leslie sighs, as though the question has been posed to her so many times before, and she is sick of explaining herself. "Short version? Jonah threw her down the basement stairs and she broke her leg. We did it before he left for Cebu with Louis. I babysat Meryl and the house while they were gone. Traipsing through Visayas, giving talks like they were God's gift to humanity. I had *no* idea what Meryl did down there the whole time. For a day or two, I sat on top of the staircase to talk to her, you know, have an actual *conversation,* for goodness' sake. I even threw her a bottle of water. We found and destroyed one CD in her bag, so I said if she told me where the other copies of the clips were, I'd give her food and painkillers. But she just kept *screaming,* so I stopped visiting. Thank you for soundproofed walls.

"When I checked up on her two weeks later, the floor looked disgusting. Feces and blood and urine everywhere. I hosed the basement down and placed her in the freezer. She was *way* lighter then. I bleached the basement floor. Burned her clothes. Pushed the cabinet so it would block the staircase. It was hard work! I nearly asked Louis for a bonus."

"You should have buried her," I say.

Leslie rolls her eyes. "Do I have to do everything around here?"

"You locked her up," Ivy says, "like an animal."

"Careful, now," Leslie says, raising the gun. Ivy shakes like a curtain caught in the wind.

"Tell her the long version, then," I say. "Once upon a time, Leslie and Meryl were classmates in Fundamental Accounting."

"Classmates in Fundamental Accounting taught by this new instructor named Jonah," Leslie continues. She smirks. "Jonah hit on Leslie at the start of the semester, thinking she would be scared and coy and demure. He was dismayed when she practically tore her clothes off for him. How am I doing with the storytelling, Professor?"

"I sense unfair subjectivity," I say. There comes a point when you feel like a figment of someone else's reality. Illusory and suspended in time. That point is now. Leslie laughs.

"So, Jonah and Leslie have sex but most of the time they hire prostitutes, male and female, to spice things up," she continues. "Then Leslie meets Mona. *Moan*-na, ha-ha. If there is a photo that accompanies the antonym of the word *coy*, you'll find a photo of Mona there, so Jonah was once again disappointed. However, he enjoyed filming the two girls, so the arrangement was satisfactory for all involved. And Mona *was* fun. At first. Then she wasn't. But the moment she stopped being fun for Leslie, she started being fun for Jonah, who liked his girls struggling and crying and practically throwing up their insides in fear. Different strokes for different folks.

"Jonah's greatest mistake was getting high and falling asleep with his laptop unlocked. Stupid piece of shit." Leslie's sudden shift to anger is unnerving, as though a black cloud has appeared in front of the sun. "Mona made a copy of the video clips and erased the copies from his hard drive. Threatened to show selected clips to the school board. It would expel me from the school and land Jonah in jail."

"You threatened her with the same thing," I say.

"She learned from the best," Leslie says. "But Mona can't handle the pressure. So, she swan-dives from the top of the Engineering building. We don't know where the disc ends up until Meryl talks to me about it. She called me first, wording her message carefully. She could have gone straight to the police but she probably thought I was a victim. So that's how I played it. I asked her to meet me at Trudy's. I shed some tears. Had a nice cinnamon roll. I told her Jonah had actually roped me into house-sitting his brother's house while they were out of town, and could we go there now? I said Jonah had more videos of naked girls kept in his room, and I wanted to help my fellow victims.

"You see, Jonah, I could be coy and demure if I wanted to.

"Louis was out doing some dumb paperwork so we had the house to ourselves. Jonah grabbed Meryl—but you know about this already."

In my head, I work out what might have happened after the brothers got back. Louis discovers the body first, confronts Jonah about it. Jonah feigns innocence. They drive out and an SUV drives them into a tree—

"For some moronic reason, Jonah didn't get rid of the body as soon as he got back, *as he was supposed to*, and now he's in a wheelchair and you're in this mess. The end." Leslie beamed at them. "Questions?"

"You're crazy," Ivy says.

"Look at this rain," says Leslie, and even I am thrown by the unexpected comment. "It is unnatural to get so much rain."

We fall silent.

"The logical thing to do during our short lives is to save this world we find ourselves in," Leslie says. "Make it at least livable. Spend our finite energy pressuring governments to focus on the environment. But the world is large. Imagine, you do your duty here, separate your fucking paper from plastic, but in another part of the planet, a company does hydraulic fracking to access natural gas under the earth, contaminating drinking water in the process and giving residents brain lesions. Chemicals are dumped in the oceans and everyone gets cancer. The logical thing to do is to fight but who has the energy to do that? How many protesters have seen change within their lifetimes? They fight, get separated from their spouses, lose custody of their children, and die poor, with the mission still unfulfilled. They move on from this world, and you wonder, what was the point of that life?

"Most people, they'd rather be rich. *Rich*. Because money is power and having power will insulate you from the world's troubles. So, you study, you work, you save, and save, and save even though a huge chunk of your salary goes to corruption. But you shrug it off, you turn a blind eye to it because the goal is to be *rich*. Once you're rich, you'll have money to protect yourself against crime and natural disasters. You'll be able to afford insurance and bodyguards and a nice house.

"Eventually, you'll move to a better country, a richer country, a country where things actually *work*.

"Then another nation detonates a nuclear bomb.

"You see? We are doomed because we are all connected. But alone, we won't survive. So we are all doomed. Even if you follow all the rules, someone, somewhere, won't, and it will be the end of you.

"If a life is defined by how it ends, then no life has meaning, Ivy, because every life ends with nothing. So, the goal, Ivy, is not to be rich or to save the planet or to help other people, but to live *now*. To find joy *now*. We are infinitesimal, Ivy. We are too small and our lives are too brief to make a difference.

There's no use making ourselves believe otherwise. Look at you: all you ever wanted was to tell Meryl how you really feel. But you decided not to tell her that because, what? It will break your Catholic mother's heart? You are afraid? Twenty years or twenty minutes from now you will be dead, and what do you get out of denying yourself what you want? Nothing. Meryl decided to take matters into her own hands because, what? A girl was wronged and justice must prevail? If she didn't get involved, she'd be alive and counting calories. And what did her involvement yield? Nothing.

"You're still living in a dream world, believing people help each other out because it's the right thing to do. You know what the true appeal of altruism is? Of *kindness?* It makes people feel good about *themselves*. Everything goes back to the self and what the self wants. Knowing this—that's not insanity, Ivy. That's being aware. That's being *awake.*"

"Are you done now?" I say, even though I feel like I am falling into a pit. I recall the 3 x 5 index card I found in Jonah's room. How strange it was. "No one wants to hear your 'big business is a sociopath' speech again."

"Ah," Leslie says. "So, a spark of Jonah remains. I'm glad. You've been weird. Why didn't you get rid of the body?"

I point at my legs. "Accident."

I can't glean anything from her expression. "Louis clearly knew about the basement. And as far as I know he has not told the police. Why didn't he bury her?"

"He didn't want to touch her." At least this is the truth.

"Goddamn pussies," Leslie says.

"I am bored now," I say, wiping my palms over my face. The perfect picture of impatience? I don't know but Leslie doesn't say anything. "Listen, my brother won't tell anyone about this because this is his house. Louis won't be able to wiggle out of this so easily. Ivy though—Ivy needs to go."

"I agree," Leslie says. "But Louis can kill you in your sleep. And then he'll go after me."

"He knew about the body, Leslie," I say. "If he were going to kill me, he'd have done it a long time ago."

"But he didn't know you were involved in Meryl's death until now. That changes things, right, Louis?"

Louis stares straight ahead and doesn't reply.

"He won't kill me, or come after you, or go to the police," I say. "You have the disc now. I believe that's the only copy around. You destroy it. The only evidence left will be the body, which, as mentioned, is in Louis's basement. He will bury the body for us and he can finally stop this philanthropic caregiver bullshit and deposit me in a hospital. Going to the police, or to Meryl's family, will only complicate things for his life. Right, Louis?"

Louis's voice is small. "Whatever you say."

"See?" I say. I try to keep my hands from trembling. "Now, about Ivy."

Ivy, crying, sits bent over her duct-taped wrists, eyes scrunched tight.

"Let's take her to the basement," I say.

27

eslie takes the disc out of the box, drops it to the floor, and steps on it. Repeatedly. The shards glitter.

"Did that feel good?" I say.

Leslie looks at me for a few seconds without saying anything. Then, she smiles. "What do we do with her?"

"First," I say, "we take her to the chest freezer and show Meryl to her."

Ivy cries.

"Then you do whatever you want. I would love to do something and teach the girl a lesson but I can't at the moment. So I guess I'll just watch." I sit back with a satisfied smile. "My crutches are in my room."

Leslie sits on the table again, cupping her chin. "Just like old times, huh," Leslie says. Her eyes disturb me.

"But with crutches this time," I say.

She laughs, tentatively at first, and then louder, slapping a hand on her knee.

"All right, wait here." She gets up and heads to my room, taking the scissors and the gun with her. Without looking back she says, "If I hear one tiny peep from any of you, I'm running back out and shooting all of you in the head."

We do as we are told. I can feel Louis's gaze burning the side of my face but I keep my eyes on my feet. I adjust the dial on my knee immobilizer and feel the pain crawl up my right thigh as my leg descends. I need to do this. I need to be able to do this.

Leslie returns with the crutches. She tries to hand me both, but I tell her to hold one for me, for now. I put weight on my left leg, using the crutch to boost me up. I straighten and my vision instantly turns gray. I crash back on the chair, hard. I hug the crutch like I would a buoy in the open ocean.

"You don't look too good," Leslie says.

"Wait," I say. The living room sways.

"I don't think I have the patience for this, Jonah."

"Just," I say, trying again, "wait." I get up, much slower. My left leg screams but it holds. I keep my other leg bent. I reach for the other crutch. Leslie hands it to me and jumps back as if I were a leper.

"There," I say, the sweat rolling down my face. "Let's go."

I am standing but I don't know how long I can stay like this.

Leslie has her gun pointed at me now. "Stay where I can see you," she says, crouching to cut the duct tape around Ivy's ankles. She leaves the scissors on the floor and yanks Ivy to her feet by her bound wrists.

"You don't trust me," I say.

"No," Leslie says. "I don't know. You seem different."

"It's just the pain."

The answer gives her pause. "You won't make it down the stairs."

"Watch me," I say.

"Insatiable until the end. Lead the way, Professor."

"See you later, Louis," I say.

"Jonah—" he starts, but I don't look back. I don't engage. I start my arduous journey to the laundry room. I imagine the pain as a small white ball on my knee, keeping it in one place, and pushing it out of the way. I hear Ivy stumbling and pleading with Leslie behind me: *Please don't, please don't do this. I won't tell anyone, please, just let me go.*

I reach the plain white door and turn the knob but can't stay on my foot long enough to unlatch it. "Get out of the way," Leslie says, pushing Ivy in front of her. The gun is aimed at Ivy's nape. Leslie reaches over to release the slide bolt latch. The door swings open.

The basement is as dark as ever. A rectangle of light coming from the laundry room falls on the landing, illuminating the splintered hulk resting there.

"You didn't even clear the cabinet?" Leslie says in indignation. I place my entire weight on the left side of my body and raise the right crutch, ready to swing at her head, until Ivy raises her arms and drives her elbow back. Leslie bends over with a grunt. Ivy steps sideways and uses her right shoulder to push Leslie into the void.

A scream, a thud, the sound of breaking wood. Ivy loses her balance and falls on the second step, which creaks beneath her. I hear Louis calling from the living room: "What's going on?"

Leslie, face bleeding, half of her body wedged inside the remains of the cabinet, cries and screams and curses. "Kill her!" she says, and I know she's talking to me. "Kill her, kill her!"

I reach over and pull Ivy to her feet. It takes three tries. Between the second and the third try Leslie lifts her gun hand and shoots. The bullet travels up the stairs and hits the door frame. Another hits the door as I slam it close.

"Jonah!" Leslie screams. I teeter on my left leg as I slide the bolt in place. "Jonah, what are you doing? Don't leave me here! Jonah, *help me!*"

"Let's go," I say. Ivy and I move back into the living room. I cannot feel my legs. I drop the crutches, fall on the couch, grab the scissors Leslie has dropped on the floor, and cut the tape around Ivy's wrists. She takes the scissors from my shaking hands and frees Louis from the chair.

Leslie is right; the soundproofing in the basement is excellent. We cannot hear her anymore.

"You did the right thing, Ivy," I say. Ivy sits on the floor, crying like an infant. Louis holds her for a while, pieces of duct tape still clinging stubbornly to his arms.

"Are you all right?" Louis asks me.

"We need to get out of here," I say.

"I need to call my brother," Ivy says, and realizes something else that makes her cry harder. "She ruined the disc! *Meryl!* She's—"

"It's all right," Louis says, stroking her magenta hair.

I must have passed out because the next time I open my eyes Louis is pushing the crutches to my chest. "One last time, Cousin," he says, placing an arm around my waist. I am on my feet again. We walk out of the house, into the rain, and into Ivy's car.

152

"Leslie is going to shoot herself," I say. My voice sounds like it's coming from very far away. "Isn't she?"

"I hope not," Louis says.

"She will," I say. I feel tears on my cheek, and I try to understand why because they don't seem connected to anything I am saying.

"Where are we going?" I ask, but I don't hear the answer. Next thing I know, we are parked somewhere indoors. Louis and someone else—*a guard?* I see a glimpse of uniform—are lowering me onto a wheelchair. I hear the guard saying "Long time, no see, sir," with cheer in his voice. I am rolled into an elevator, down a hallway, and into a dark, musty room.

"Where—" But I think I know where. Louis turns on the lights and draws the curtains. I see that I am in a living room with a leather couch and a huge TV. I look out the window. Jonah's apartment has a good view of the city. Good, because everything looks so far away. The rain has stopped, and the stars are starting to come out.

Louis hands me a glass of water. I hear him opening doors, trying the keys on anything that's locked. I drink the water and only then realize how thirsty I am. "Jonah lives here," I say, and Louis says yes.

He is gone for some time. When he comes back, he sits on the couch and says, "There is a small room at the end of the corridor. I thought it was a storage closet. There is an old desktop computer in there. Photos." Louis looks like he is going to throw up. "Discs."

I take a deep breath. *Of course.* I nod. *I see.*

Louis says, "I sent Ivy a message. I told her to give us an hour before calling the police."

154

He places two bottles of mineral water and four prescription bottles on the glass-top table in front of the couch. The bottles bear Jonah's name and the generic names of the pills within: hydrocodone, diazepam, temazepam, and alprazolam. Painkillers. Anti-anxiety. Sleeping aids.

I think of my sister. *Our parents' love has a hard edge to it.* Celeste said that, before Uncle Pedro ruined her. *They cherish us at arm's length,* she said, and think of our inevitable deaths not with anger and denial in their hearts but with a calm acceptance. Because there is a power greater than our life force. Because we dwell in borrowed bodies. Because nothing is ours.

If you die now, Celeste said, *I will be furious. You deserve to have someone in your life who will say,* This is not okay. *You deserve to have someone who will be angry when you die.*

I have gone past anger, but no, no, this is not okay.

"I am so sorry, Louis," I say.

"I'm sorry, too," Louis says. "I wish things would end a different way. But here we are."

These are the ways we can escape this mess: find another body, or go back home and hope the family will accept us once again.

But I am so tired.

Pain is bad for the heart, my mother used to say.

"I wish I could sleep," I say.

What I wish, really, is to turn back Time.

Louis opens the prescription bottles. "We can start with the alprazolam," he says, taking a handful of pills and passing them to me.

"What do you think comes after?" he says. "Or is that a pointless question to ask?"

Nothing. What follows is what came before we were born—nothing.

And that is all right, Celeste.

"Still here?" Louis says, peering at my face.

"I think," I say. I glance out the window. The sky is starting to change color. Is it morning already?

Louis has opened one bottle of mineral water. The pills sit on the palm of his hand, white and sharp, like teeth.

I suddenly remember my twin brothers, pushing me out of the kitchen and laughing.

I reach out and place a hand on Louis's arm.

There is a knock on the door. Faint. Tentative. Perhaps it is Auntie, finding us again, and for the last time. Perhaps a neighbor, or Ivy, or the cops. Perhaps my mother. Perhaps there is mercy in the end, after all. "Wait," I tell both the door and Louis.

Wait.

Acknowledgments

I would like to thank, once again, Ms. Nida, Kyra, and the rest of the Visprint team for the love and attention they gave to this book.

My thanks to the readers for their support and words of encouragement.

I am grateful to be surrounded by loving, entertaining people (who are entertaining enough to give me inspiration for my stories) and for this I would like to thank my parents and my siblings, the Lazarte family, and my friends.

My love and thanks to Jaykie, constant companion.

And I would like to thank you, Dear Reader, who is holding this book now — I hope you enjoyed (will enjoy) reading this tale.

Eliza Victoria
Makati City, May 2014

Published by Tuttle Publishing, an imprint of Periplus Editions (HK) Ltd

www.tuttlepublishing.com

Copyright © 2014 Eliza Victoria
www.elizavictoria.com

First published in the Philippines in
2014 by Visprint, Inc.

Published by Tuttle Publishing in 2022

Library of Congress Control Number:
2022931249

ISBN: 978-0-8048-5523-5

First edition
25 24 23 22
6 5 4 3 2 1

Printed in Malaysia
2205TO

Distributed by
North America, Latin America
& Europe
Tuttle Publishing
364 Innovation Drive
North Clarendon, VT 05759-9436 U.S.A.
Tel: 1 (802) 773-8930
Fax: 1 (802) 773-6993
info@tuttlepublishing.com
www.tuttlepublishing.com

Japan
Tuttle Publishing
Yaekari Building 3rd Floor
5-4-12 Osaki
Shinagawa-ku
Tokyo 141-0032
Tel: (81) 3 5437-0171
Fax: (81) 3 5437-0755
sales@tuttle.co.jp
www.tuttle.co.jp

Asia Pacific
Berkeley Books Pte. Ltd.
3 Kallang Sector #04-01
Singapore 349278
Tel: (65) 6741-2178
Fax: (65) 6741-2179
inquiries@periplus.com.sg
www.tuttlepublishing.com

"Books to Span the East and West"